# Joanna's Journey

# Joanna's Journey

Audrey Hopkins

**Scripture Union**
130 City Road, London EC1V 2NJ

© Audrey Hopkins 1990
First published 1990

ISBN 0 86201 580 4

All rights reserved. No part of this publication may be reproduced, stored in a retrieval system, or transmitted, in any form or by any means, electronic, mechanical, photocopying, recording or otherwise, without the prior permission of Scripture Union.

Phototypeset by Input Typesetting Ltd, London
Printed and bound in Great Britain by Cox and Wyman Ltd, Reading

# Chapter One

Joanna twisted her ankles round the chair legs and leaned forward at her desk. She propped her head on her hands so that her arms made an upside-down grey woolly 'V' with her chin at the point. She watched Mr Brown pick up his dark-rimmed spectacles and perch them on top of his crinkly black hair before he leaned on the book-case behind his desk. She could see his white shirt through his cardigan sleeve. Leaning on the same spot every day had worn the wool thin where his bony elbow rested and she supposed it stayed that way because he didn't have a wife to darn it or patch it with a piece of leather like the Headmaster's wife did for him.

It was her favourite part of the day when all the arithmetic and science was done and home-time was only twenty minutes away. Mr Brown enjoyed it too. He loved books and shared his pleasure in them with his class, reading aloud and bringing the characters to life as he changed his voice and accent for each one.

He never minded stopping to explain a word or read a special bit a second time.

Joanna felt a warm glow inside as she settled deeper into her seat.

'What is it to be today then?' Mr Brown asked. 'Who is going to be the lucky one?'

A dozen hands shot up, all eager to hear their own favourite. Joanna didn't mind what Mr Brown read. Everything was so good that she would be quite happy if he read the thirteen-times table out loud. She had been chosen to sing the part of Mary in the play 'Christmas Jazz' that the fourth year were presenting at the end of term and was so thrilled that it showed in her sparkling eyes and happy grin.

'And just what is tickling *you*, Joanna Lacey? You look like the kitten who had the top of the milk for his supper!'

Joanna blushed.

'I'm singing in the school play, sir – solo!' she said in a low voice.

'Well done! Mrs Boswell told me she was holding auditions. Who else has got a part?'

Several hands went up and Mr Brown's smile widened.

'What a talented class I have. *Now!*' he cried suddenly, making everybody jump and giggle. '*Who..who..who?*'

His eyes were on the class, darting here and there to make his choice. Martin Simms' carrot-coloured hair caught his attention and he pointed.

'*You!*'

'Pirates, sir . . . and the Spanish Main,' Martin cried as he brandished his ruler aloft and jabbed at an imagin-

6

ary foe.

'Pirates it is, then,' Mr Brown agreed, bending down to the third shelf and choosing a book with a bright cover. There was a moment of panic while, as always, he searched for his spectacles and the class told him loudly, 'On your head, sir!' Then he perched on the empty desk in front of Joanna and began.

He read aloud with lots of 'Yo-ho-hos' and 'Aha, Jim lads'. The whole class were laughing so much that their eyes were full of tears and Martin fell off his chair to add to the fun. Mr Sumner, the headmaster, opened the classroom door and rang the big bell, shaking his shiny bald head at all the noise.

'4A making themselves heard again?' he asked sternly, but his eyes were twinkling under his bushy white brows. He knew how much Mr Brown's stories were enjoyed.

There was silence as they stood at their desks for end-of-the-day prayers though; for as Mr Brown always said, 'There is a time and a place for everything'.

'Thank you, God, for the gift of laughter and for the written word,' Mr Brown began.

And thank you for my part in the play. I'm so glad I can sing and that Mrs Boswell liked me, Joanna prayed silently.

'Amen,' said Mr Brown.

'Amen,' said 4A, no-one more meaningfully than Joanna Lacey.

It was quite cold outside and the three girls pulled up the hoods of their duffle coats and thrust their hands deep into the big square pockets.

'Brrrr,' said Joanna to her friends, Anne and Cathy, as they walked down the hill towards the town centre.

'Brrrr. I hope the bonfire is a big one. We'll need it to keep us warm tonight.'

'We're having a little one in our garden. Mum says our Brian's too little to be out in the cold. I wish I was going to the park with you two, though. Dad's bought a box of fireworks, the pretty ones, but it won't be the same,' Anne said, pulling her mouth down at the corners to make a sad face.

Joanna gave Anne's arm a squeeze as they all said goodbye at the main road. Anne went to the left towards the bus station for her ride out to the new housing estate at the edge of the town and Cathy turned right to the rows of old brick terraces behind the market-place. Joanna crossed at the pelican crossing and was soon at the block of flats in the town centre.

Pavilion Mansions. The black and gold sign-board was lit by a neon tube and the ground floor hallway was thickly carpeted right to the row of lifts at the far end. Joanna never used the lift when she was on her own in case it stopped with her stuck inside. She had always hated small spaces, even the Wendy house at infant school.

There were two letters in the Lacey mailbox and Joanna collected them, using the small key that hung with the bigger door key from a pink plastic spiral attached to her waistband. It only took a minute to reach her floor by the left staircase and open the door to 3B. Joanna always felt very grown up when she unlocked the door and let herself in. Anne and Cathy *never* had their own keys because their mothers were always at home. The Lacey family had moved house quite often but Joanna and her mother had lived in this rather nice apartment for almost three years. Daddy appeared every now and then, on leave from his overseas work as an engineer, and once Joanna and her mother had travelled to Riyadh in the Middle East to spend a holiday with him. Joanna had come back nut-brown and full of stories and had kept the class interested for days and days.

Mrs Lacey was still out. The high school, where she taught English, was across the town beyond the new ring-road and finished fifteen minutes after St Mark's junior school, where Joanna went. One of the letters from the mailbox was a bill, so that went into the letter-rack on the bookcase and the other, for Mrs Lacey, was placed on the kitchen table by the bowl of roses she had bought at the weekend.

Joanna moved a fallen petal from the shiny table top and popped it into the waste bin under the sink before she went into her bedroom. By the time she had changed into her jeans and a thick woolly jumper she heard her mother's key rattle in the lock and ran to meet her, carrying her boots in her hand.

'Have you hung up your uniform?' Mrs Lacey asked, after she had dumped a carrier bag full of exercise books on the table and given Joanna a big hug.

Joanna grinned . . . every night the same question! She watched with dismay as coffee cups were taken from their hooks and the kettle was switched on.

'We're not having tea, are we?' she cried. 'I thought we were going straight away and having hot-dogs?'

Mrs Lacey perched on a tall stool at the breakfast bar, one toe on the floor and her other foot on the metal cross-frame.

'Let me get my breath!' she said with a grin. 'A cup of coffee isn't going to take long.'

Joanna climbed onto the other bar stool, her own feet dangling quite a long way from the floor.

'Will I be as tall as you when I grow up?' she asked, swinging her legs either side of the stool.

Mrs Lacey sipped her coffee.

'We're both blond and blue-eyed . . . and people say you have my nose, so it's quite likely you'll be long and thin too! And Daddy's taller than me so I hardly think you'll be shrimp sized!'

The cups were washed, dried and back on their hooks before the pair set off towards the bus station, window-shopping along Market Street as they went the long way round. Joanna loved window-shopping with her mother. Together they planned outfits and created colour schemes for bedrooms and kitchens, planning for the day they would have a house in the country, choosing curtains and crockery and even tea-towels to match for their new home when Daddy was back for good. They paused for a moment at the bookshop to look at the display of new titles and spent a long time at the big windows of the town's largest department store.

Joanna slipped her arm through her mother's as they crossed to the bus station. The 'Grand Bonfire and Firework Display' was at Moor park on the northern edge of the town. Joanna looked for Cathy at the clock tower where they had arranged to meet. She was easy to spot for she was wearing her bright yellow anorak with its fluorescent bands and was shining more brightly than the fireworks! The fire was well alight by seven o'clock and by half past it was roaring almost twelve feet high. The fireworks were spectacular and the hot dogs and baked potatoes quite delicious. Joanna and Cathy strolled arm in arm around the bonfire, always keeping a sharp eye on their parents who were standing together talking.

'I'm glad you got a part in the play too,' Joanna said as she wiped her buttery fingers on a red paper napkin. 'And Anne too – we're all so lucky!'

Cathy nodded, her mouth too full of her third hot dog to answer straight away. She was to sing the part of the donkey that carried Mary to Bethlehem; a merry little song that began '*Clip, Clop*' and suited her low voice and comic personality.

'I have to dance too!' she said when she had emptied her mouth of a mustardy bit of sausage. 'So that's great!'

Joanna nodded and grinned. She had already seen Cathy waggle her hips and shake the school tie she had pinned on her P.T. shorts as a donkey's tail. Cathy was the class clown, her bright red hair and freckly face always in the middle of any fun.

A huge rocket whooshed into the sky and burst, scattering red and green stars in a cascade over the town. There were speeches by the mayor and other important guests, thanking all those who had made the evening possible, then Joanna's mother called her to go home. Joanna felt proud of her mother as she neared the group of parents. She looked so much younger than the others in her shiny white car coat and matching trilby hat. It perched on the smooth hair that Mrs Lacey piled on top of her head and had a red leather band exactly the colour of her red high-heeled boots.

Cathy's plump little mum was beaming as the two girls joined them.

'You look more like your mum every time I see you, Joanna!' she said, when they were close enough.

Joanna stood at least another inch taller. That was just what she wanted . . . to look *exactly* like her mother. She was easily as tall as Cathy's mum when she lifted her heels a little bit.

'Cathy is a good friend, isn't she?' Mrs Lacey observed as they waited for the bus.

Joanna nodded. 'And Anne too. We'll all be in your class when we come to the high school, won't we?' she asked. 'Cathy thinks that you are absolutely fantastic!'

Mrs Lacey smiled. 'We'll see!' she said.

They had to wait some time for a bus. When it came it was full of screaming children, their mothers ignoring their noise. Joanna sat quietly beside her mother until they reached the bus station. It was almost nine-thirty when they reached Pavilion Mansions and this time Joanna ran to press the button to call the lift. She didn't mind riding in it when her mother was there too.

'Get ready for bed, Joanna, and I'll bring you a milky drink,' Mrs Lacey said, hurrying across the lounge and through the archway into the kitchen area.

Joanna washed her hands and face in the bathroom, then sat at her dressing table to brush her hair. In the mirror she could see her bedroom. It was warm and cosy and prettily pink and white. She had chosen the curtains and matching duvet cover herself from a catalogue and they did look nice against the rose-pink walls and white woodwork. The radiator under the window kept the room nice and warm. She shivered when she thought of the night she had spent at Cathy's house. How cold it had been in Cathy's tiny bedroom.

She looked at herself in the mirror. Her straight fair hair was parted in the middle and now that it wasn't held by an elastic band it hung down each side of her face and onto her shoulders.

'Why can't I have curly hair like Anne?' she asked her own pale face in the mirror. 'And rosy cheeks like Cathy?'

'Because you're you and not Anne or Cathy!' Mrs Lacey said, coming into the room with two steaming mugs and a plate of chocolate digestive biscuits balanced on top of one of them. 'And it wouldn't do for everybody to be the same! Into bed with you now.'

Just as they were settling down for a bedtime chat the telephone rang. Mrs Lacey hurried to answer it.

'That will be Daddy,' she said. 'He said he would call on bonfire night. You have a little read while I talk to him. I'll call you to say goodnight.'

Joanna took her favourite book from the shelf and climbed into bed, propping up the pillows behind her and making her knees into a mountain. It was a big book and it needed her knees for support. Sometimes she read *The House at Pooh Corner* as a change from school books and adventure stories but tonight she was looking for something really special.

There! Page twenty-three. The picture of Mary in her blue gown and white head-dress smiled at her from the shiny page and opposite were written the words she was to sing in the school play. She read the story first, how an angel had told the young woman about the baby she was going to have, and then she read all the words of the song called the Magnificat, very carefully.

'My soul doth magnify the Lord, and my spirit hath rejoiced in God my Saviour.'

She didn't know the tune yet so was reading the words for the second time when her mother called her to the phone.

'Hello Daddy!' she said into the receiver. 'How are you? I'm going to sing solo in the school play!'

'That is good news, Joanna. What part is it?'

Joanna told her father all about the auditions and the song she was to sing, talking very fast and not breathing at all until his laughter brought her to a stop.

'You're excited!' he said. 'And so you should be. I'm very pleased that you were chosen to sing such beautiful words. I wish I could be there to hear them.'

'Does that mean you won't be here for Christmas?' Joanna wailed, all the joy gone from her voice.

'I'm afraid not,' Mr Lacey went on. 'But Mummy will tell you all about it and I'll be thinking of you on the night of the play. God bless, Joanna. Remember, he will be listening.'

'Goodnight, Daddy, and God bless. Here's Mummy again.'

As Joanna climbed back into bed she remembered those last words, 'He will be listening'. She picked up her book of Bible stories and turned the pages until she came to one she especially liked, Jesus the shepherd, holding a tiny lamb in his arms. Daddy was right. Jesus always listened to people's troubles, so it wasn't unusual to suppose that he would be listening to her song.

'What did Daddy say you would tell me about?' she asked when her mother had settled on the end of her bed again.

'It's big news, Joanna. He's been transferred to the Far East – to Singapore.'

'Are we going for a holiday?'

Mrs Lacey collected both mugs and walked to the door before she spoke again.

'No, Joanna. He wants us to go and live there.'

She was stunned, kneeling up in bed with no thought at all for her precious book that fell with a loud 'clunk' onto the bedside rug.

'For good?'

'Well . . . for quite some time, anyway.'

'You mean leave here? Leave this lovely house and all my friends? We can't do that – it would be too awful!' Joanna squeaked, her voice rising with each sentence until it was little more than a whisper.

'I like it here too, Joanna – but I'm sure I'll like Singapore just as much. Daddy says it's like one big garden and just think, it's always summer!' Mrs Lacey put down the mugs on the bedside table and picked up the book, checking the spine for damage.

'But what about Anne and Cathy?'

'Anne and Cathy will think it's a great adventure and you'll be the envy of everyone at school, leaving all this cold and rain. Now go and clean your teeth. It's time you were asleep!'

Mrs Lacey disappeared with the mugs and Joanna ran to the bathroom.

'I don't want an adventure,' she told herself in the mirror. 'I want to be Mary and sing in church on Christmas Eve, and I want my friends and my nice house and . . .'

She was crying now and the tears were getting all mixed up in the toothpaste.

'You can still sing at school,' her mother said from the bathroom doorway. 'We won't go until the end of term.'

Joanna rinsed her mouth and walked slowly back to bed.

'But what about church?' she said, still sniffing as she

pushed her toes to the bottom and wriggled them against the cool cotton sheets.

'We'll talk about that tomorrow, Joanna. It's late.'

'But I don't want to . . .' she began, but stopped as something in her mother's face told her to stop arguing and say goodnight. It wasn't an angry face; it was more of a sad face and it puzzled Joanna quite a lot.

Perhaps Mummy doesn't want to go either, she thought. And tomorrow she'll call Daddy and tell him and everything will be right again. Daddy can go and we'll stay here, like always, just the two of us.

'Goodnight, Joanna,' Mrs Lacey said as she turned out the light.

'Goodnight, Mummy. See you in the morning,' Joanna answered. She squeezed her eyes tight shut and clasped her hands together under her chin. Daddy had reminded her that Jesus always listens to those who talk to him and she had a lot to say.

'Please, Jesus,' she prayed. 'Keep us safe through the night and look after the world tomorrow and . . .'

She paused, opening her eyes just a little to peer at her bedroom by the light of the street lamp filtering through her curtains. The smooth pink walls were reflected in the mirror on her dressing table and just to the right of the mirror her special treasures – the green satin snake that Daddy had brought from Texas and a camel with two humps from Egypt, a Japanese fan and a jade egg – were squashed between a variety of small creatures, all fluffy, all four-legged and very much loved.

'And *please*, if at all possible, let me stay here where everything is lovely. Amen.'

# Chapter Two

It was very foggy and Joanna imagined herself lost in a mysterious world as she made her way to the corner. The monsters that approached her turned out to be Anne and Cathy who joined her for the long trudge up the hill to school.

'Ooh, isn't it horrid!' Anne said, pulling an equally horrid face.

Cathy didn't say anything because she couldn't. Her long scarf was wrapped around her face so many times that only her eyes were showing and they were half closed against the fog.

Joanna grunted 'Hello', and the three tramped on in silence. She stopped pretending to be an explorer and tried to make some sense of her feelings and thoughts. Mummy had been quiet at breakfast and Joanna had pushed the scrambled egg around her plate until... She heaved a sigh as she remembered the breakfast conversation.

'Daddy is really looking forward to us all being together, Joanna. He feels very lonely so far away.'

'I don't care how he feels!'

She had been sorry almost at once. Her mother's face had gone white then red. 'We'll talk about it tonight.'

Joanna had felt mean and miserable as she left the flat and the feeling had not gone away. She had to squeeze her eyes tightly to stop her tears.

'Why have you got your eyes shut?' Cathy mumbled through four layers of wool.

'There's nothing to see, so why don't you mind your own business!' Joanna snapped.

Both girls stopped walking in amazement at Joanna's outburst, then she bit her lip and stopped too, a few paces in front of them.

'What's the matter with you this morning?' Anne asked the rigid back in front of her. 'Is it something *we've* done?' Her hands were on her hips and she was ready for battle. Although Cathy had the red hair it was Anne who had the short temper.

Cathy said nothing. Her happy face, so often full of fun, had paled at Joanna's words and she set off again, passing her friend in silence, her eyes fixed on her feet.

Joanna felt sick inside. They were all good friends but Cathy was really special. She ran to catch up and linked arms with Cathy then turned to hold out a hand to Anne before she spoke.

'I'm sorry,' she said quietly. 'I didn't mean to be horrid but I've had some awful news!'

'Can you tell us about it . . . or is it very private?' Cathy asked.

Joanna felt terrible. Anne was angry with her but she knew that Cathy was remembering her own unhappiness just a year ago; when her father had left a few days before Christmas. She was over it now and visited him and his new wife occasionally but it still hurt.

'Daddy's been transferred to Singapore and we're going to live there – before Christmas!'

There was a stunned silence.

'That's China, isn't it?' Anne ventured, just for something to say.

Joanna shook her head. 'I don't think so,' she sobbed.

'Mr Brown will tell you where it is,' Cathy suggested as they turned into the playground.

'I don't *care* where it is. I don't want to *go*!' Joanna gasped, breaking free and running into the building without looking back.

'Well! What do you think of that?' Anne asked her friend.

'I don't think I'd like it, Anne,' Cathy replied as she unwound her scarf. 'I wouldn't like it at all!'

Mr Brown pulled out the big map of the world that he kept rolled up behind the blackboard. It was very old and cracked in places so that sometimes it was difficult to read a name or see exactly where a river ran. The last time the big map came out was when Joanna was going to Riyadh and Mr Brown had pointed it out to the class.

'This old thing only sees daylight when Joanna's off to foreign parts,' he said, blowing the dust off and pinning it to the wooden edge of the blackboard. 'It's a bit out of date, though. Look at all the red bits! They were all part of the British Empire once.'

The class gathered round and listened, every eye on the map.

'Now then,' Mr Brown began. 'This is us – here!' He pointed to the British Isles with a long ruler. 'And this is China, right over on the other side. This is Malaya . . . oops! Sorry, it's called Malaysia now . . . and here, right at the tip, is the small island of Singapore.'

'It's a long, long way,' Cathy said, her hand tracing a line, in the air above her, right across Russia, over the Himalayas and down the long finger of land to the tiny island at its tip.

Joanna didn't want to look at the map. She didn't want to believe it was all happening but once Mr Brown started talking he held them all spellbound, even Joanna.

'What excitement, Joanna,' he said. 'Just think of all the things you'll see and the people you'll meet.'

The lesson developed into a talk about Malaysia and rubber plantations; about Chinese foods and customs and all the things that would have excited Joanna if it wasn't going to be happening to her.

It made her miserable. I have everything I want right here, she told herself.

By lunch time she was in a very bad mood and ate her packed lunch alone. Anne and Cathy had school dinner, so she couldn't eat with them anyway and she avoided everyone else. There was a rehearsal at half past twelve and she had to pull herself together for that.

For, she told herself, you don't want to lose *that* too!

She sang well and Mrs Boswell beamed at her over the little half spectacles that sat on the end of her nose.

'Oh, Joanna!' she praised. 'You do have a lovely voice and you are picking up the tune so quickly!'

Joanna was glad there was no-one else in the room; she would have been so embarrassed. She did manage a smile and a nod then began again as the piano gave her the tune to learn. It was a difficult piece and learning it took her mind off everything else for the rest of the dinner hour.

The afternoon dragged on and even Mr Brown, who could make long division exciting, held no interest for Joanna. All she could think of were the words she had said to Anne and Cathy that morning.

'*I don't care!*' She had never used those words before today and yet she'd said them to her best friends *and* to her mother at breakfast. The awful thing was that she meant them! She didn't care if it was warm and beautiful in Singapore, or about what a *very* lucky girl she was to be having such an adventure! She was quite content in foggy old England!

The bell went for afternoon play and she hurried out to find a quiet corner. It wasn't easy. It was rather cold and everybody was running about and making a lot of noise. At last she pressed herself into the corner where the teachers' room jutted out at the side of the building. She could hear them talking and laughing but the words were just a jumble. She was huddled there feeling really miserable when a plastic football hit her legs. The corners of her mouth turned down even more when a group of small boys charged into her hiding place scrambling for their ball. Joanna kicked it as hard as she could and it soared over the side wall and down the hill.

'What did you do that for?' the leader of the pack yelled.

Joanna stuck her nose in the air and strode past them.

'Why did you do it?' Anne asked, taking her by the arm to stop her. 'It wasn't very kind to lose their ball!'

'I don't care about their stupid ball!'

There! She had said it again!

With a little cry Joanna dashed for the side door and

ran into the cloakroom, straight into Mrs Stubbs who was on duty.

'What are you doing in here, Joanna Lacey? You should be out in the yard!'

Joanna just couldn't answer and the more Miss Stubbs demanded a reply the more Joanna stuck out her lip and refused.

'Very well, then. I know you like Mr Brown's stories at the end of the day so you can tidy out my cupboard instead!' Miss Stubbs decided.

The last lesson was a disaster, with Joanna worried about what her mother would say if Miss Stubbs told about her behaviour and Mr Brown very concerned about her miserable face and seeming lack of interest. Story time came and Joanna cleaned the dusty cupboard instead.

It's not my fault! she thought. *They* have spoilt everything for me. Nobody understands!

By the time she had finished with Miss Stubbs and her cupboard everybody else had gone. Anne had a bus to catch and Cathy had gone with her. Joanna didn't blame them for leaving her to walk home alone. She had been so unlike herself all day and she hadn't been pleasant company. She walked straight past Pavilion Mansions, knowing her mother wouldn't be home yet and wishing that just once she could arrive home and find the table full of cakes and pastries fresh from the oven and her mother's face glowing from a coal fire. Cathy did!

Almost defiantly and ignoring her mother's orders she walked on into the town centre with its busy rush hour streets and crowded stores.

Crossing the road was difficult and twice Joanna's

heart beat faster when a car horn made her jump. She walked right through one of the big department stores without really seeing anything, coming out at a different place and entering another store almost immediately. Suddenly she became aware of a tall man in a dark suit tapping his foot impatiently at a set of double doors and she realised he was waiting to close the store. Red-faced, she hurried outside to find herself right down by the river. She heard the Town Hall clock strike six and panicked. She had been wandering about for nearly two hours and was right across town from Pavilion Mansions. She knew her mother would be frantic. She walked as quickly as she could, keeping to the well-lit main roads, the lighted shop windows holding no interest for her now. She was thankful that the clock, heard all over the town, didn't strike the next hour and she burst into the apartment at twenty minutes to seven.

There was no anger. Mrs Lacey gave a cry of relief and hugged her, then asked where on earth she had been.

There were a great many tears, most of them from Joanna herself who was really sorry she had been so stupid.

'But I was quite safe,' she insisted. 'And I know my way all round the town!'

'That's not the point,' her mother said. 'The worry was mine because I didn't know you were safe. You must always think of the other people involved, Joanna – and how your actions affect them!'

After the dried-up sausages and mash had been eaten and the tea things were finally cleared away, Mrs Lacey called Joanna to sit beside her on the settee. She explained very carefully that Daddy had to go where his company sent him. They made electronic equipment for aircraft and he travelled with new inventions to train the operators to use and repair them. Daddy had always worked away for as long as Joanna could remember.

'Daddy and I have only been together for holidays and when he's been between contracts ever since you were born,' her mother went on. 'And we didn't mind, because *you* were important. We wanted a stable home life for you, not travelling here and there every few months. And the Middle East was no place to take a new baby. This is the third time Daddy has been to Riyadh. We could have gone to live there two years ago but you were so happy at school.'

'And I still am!' Joanna cried.

'Yes . . . but you would be starting high school after the summer so things would be changing anyway. It really is a good time to make the move.'

Mrs Lacey put an arm around Joanna's shoulder and cuddled her. Joanna sighed. Was she being selfish?

They watched television together for a little while, then Mrs Lacey moved to sit at the table, opening the first of a set of English exercise books, her red pencil at the ready. Joanna got out the song she would be singing in the school play and tried to concentrate on the words and music, but the notes kept jumping about and she lost her place so many times that she gave up and closed her eyes. It was over a year since the visit to Riyadh and Daddy had been home once since then. Most of the time Joanna had either been in school or in bed. She could remember the outings they had, like Chester Zoo where she had held a baby orang-outang and Wigan Pier with the museum called 'The Way we Were'. The Victorian school-room had been the highlight of that visit, a lesson in what school used to be like. Joanna could picture the actor, who had played the stern schoolmaster so well that she'd trembled when he'd asked her a question. She could even see the face of the baby ape in her mind's eye but, with growing dismay, she found it very difficult to picture Daddy at all! His face would vanish, or turn into Mr Brown just when she thought she had it.

Joanna crept to the cupboard under the bookshelves and found the big photograph album that lived there. Without disturbing her mother she settled at the table opposite her. Flicking through the stiff cardboard pages she noticed that most of the photographs were of herself and Mummy — Mummy and Joanna in the park, Mummy and Joanna on the swings, Joanna and Mummy on a donkey, Mummy and . . .

It made her think.

Daddy appeared now and again — in his Air Force uniform, holding his baby daughter in his arms, but never a part of Joanna's fun. She felt a little uncomfortable. It would make her mother very happy and it would be nice to be a family. The album pictures would have three people in them . . . having fun! In her comfy bed with all the day's troubles behind her, Joanna promised herself and Jesus that she would try to be happy about the move.

'. . . and help me to think of others as Jesus did. I was horrid to Anne and Cathy and spiteful to the boys with the ball and I made my mother unhappy when I didn't come straight home from school. I haven't been at all like myself today. Help me to think of others instead of always thinking of myself, and keep us all safe this night especially Daddy so far away across the sea. Amen.'

Saturday was an ordinary sort of day. Mrs Lacey cleaned the flat in the morning and Joanna did the dusting. It was her Saturday job and earned her a magazine from the newsagents on the corner. In the afternoon the pair did the weekly shopping and Singapore wasn't mentioned at all, though six pairs of white cotton socks went into the shopping bag, a reminder of the journey to come. Joanna tried not to think about them. The public library was the last place on the list and was one of Joanna's favourite places. She hurried into the junior section while her mother handed in the books and collected the tickets. The shelves were as exciting as the Christmas shop windows to Joanna and her blond head bobbed up and down among them as she tried to choose between so many.

'Come on, bookworm!' her mother whispered from the arch that led to the adult section. 'It's closing time in ten minutes.'

Joanna looked up from her cross-legged position on the floor.

'I wish I could take them all!' she said.

The librarian smiled as she stamped the books.

'My favourites too,' she said.

Joanna clutched the first two of the Narnia books under one arm and waited for her third choice to be stamped.

'How many times have you read those?' her mother asked with a smile. Although she had asked the question she didn't really need an answer. She understood that some books are just as exciting the second, third and even fourth time of reading.

'When I was little,' she told Joanna as they travelled

the two bus stops to Pavilion Mansions, 'I had a book called *Purl and Plain*. It was about two knitted dolls and their adventures. It was the first *full* book I managed to read all by myself. I kept it with me even when I went to university.'

'Where is it now?' Joanna asked.

Mrs Lacey lifted her shoulders in a sad way.

'Somebody took it,' she said quietly. 'But I forgave them, because if they needed it *that* much perhaps it would be treasured as I had treasured it.'

Joanna wished she could be as kind as her mother.

'I hope nobody takes my *Pooh Corner*!' she said.

After a long bath and a hot chocolate drink Joanna went to her room to have a read before going to sleep. She didn't have to be up quite so early in the morning because church and Sunday school didn't begin until ten-thirty. She was the youngest member of the church choir and felt very proud when she took part in an anthem on special occasions, or sang one of the descants Mr Coombes arranged for the sopranos. She snuggled down in bed and considered her books. She picked up *The Lion, the Witch and the Wardrobe* and put it down again. That was a book to read on a wet afternoon when it was too nasty to go out and she could lose herself in the magical land of Narnia. Instead, she chose the book she had taken from the biography section.

'*The Small Woman*,' she read aloud. 'The story of Gladys Aylward.'

It was a book about a young woman who wanted to go to China to tell the story of Jesus to the people in remote villages. It was a children's version with lots of pictures and Joanna was soon involved in the young Gladys's struggle to get to China. When her eyes were tired she looked at the pictures further on in the book. She didn't like the drawing of little people bundled up in what looked like rags, or the sketch of a woman's foot, bound up in bandages from childhood to keep it small. How horrid it looked without the wrappings and how painful it must have been for the poor woman!

Long after her mother had turned out the light Joanna lay thinking about the Small Woman and her life in China.

'But she *wanted* to go,' she told herself. 'And I don't.'

# Chapter Three

The fog had lifted and the pale wintry sun shone through the coloured glass window behind the table. Joanna couldn't see the window from her seat in the choir stalls, but the colours were reflected in the silver candlesticks and the tall brass lectern at the head of the nave. She could see her mother sitting halfway down the church, all by herself in the pew. Most of the other people were sitting in family groups – mother, father and children – with, in some pews, granny and grandad too!

Mrs Cooper sat alone as did Mrs Farrier and Mr Greaves but they were much older than Joanna's mother. It was sad that she should be away from Daddy. Why did life have to be so complicated?

The service was coming to an end and the congregation were singing the last hymn, the choir providing a descant over the tune. Mrs Lacey waved as she left the pew and walked up the aisle to the west door where the Reverend Stocks was waiting to shake hands with everybody and wish them well. Joanna liked him a lot.

He was always joking and making the young people laugh and it was he who dressed up as Santa to hand out presents at Christmas.

Joanna gulped as she remembered that she wouldn't be at the Sunday school party this year and at that moment the sun went behind a cloud and all the light and colours faded. It made her miserable again. She stood at the church door and watched her mother disappear round the corner, hurrying home to cook Sunday lunch while Joanna went to Sunday school.

It took less than two minutes to walk across the churchyard to the parish rooms next to the vicarage. Joanna made her usual stop at a small headstone just off the main path.

'We're going to Singapore,' she said quietly. Her grandmother was a very vague memory of gingerbread men and a pretty garden and just one old brown photograph in the album. She was the only grandparent Joanna had known. Daddy's parents had died when he was a little boy and Grandad Brooks, her mother's father, had died in North Africa in the war. She knew that Grandma Brooks was not 'there' in the churchyard but the stone did provide a link and she always felt good there.

Joanna loved Sunday school. She enjoyed singing the jolly songs that Kelly-Ann Johns taught her class and was always ready to hear the Bible stories time and time again. Joanna had planned to be a Sunday school teacher, just like Kelly-Ann, when she was old enough. Now it seemed unlikely. Her mother had said only that morning that when they came back from the Far East in a few years time, they would find a cottage in a pretty village and settle down for good. The cottage was a nice thought but Joanna would have liked home to be here, right in town.

This Sunday Kelly-Ann told the story of Joseph and his brothers – how they were jealous of him and sold him into slavery in Egypt. Kelly-Ann played a tape after the story, of Joseph singing about his coat of many colours. Joanna couldn't help the tears that trickled down her cheeks as she listened to the music and drew Joseph in his coloured coat.

'Whatever is the matter?' Kelly-Ann asked. 'It all turns out fine in the end, you know!'

Joanna gulped and tried to smile.

'I know how Joseph felt!' she explained. She went on to tell Kelly-Ann and the class about her coming journey to a strange land. As she listed all the things she would miss, like Sunday school, the choir, Kelly-Ann and even Gran's grave, the tears fell and she sobbed.

Kelly-Ann put an arm round her shoulder and was quiet for a minute. Everybody else just sat, not knowing what to do.

'What an adventure!' the young teacher said when Joanna's shoulders had almost stopped shaking. 'I hope you'll write and tell us all about it . . . and send lots of photographs.'

'I don't want to go,' Joanna sniffed, wiping her eyes with a tissue provided by her comforter. 'I want to stay here and sing in the choir and have Christmas and everything. I want to be a Sunday school teacher when I'm old enough and . . .'

Kelly-Ann stopped her with a finger on her lips.

'Joseph didn't want to go to Egypt,' she said. 'But he made the best of it and became a very important man. So important that he was able to save his father *and* his brothers when they needed him. You are important too, Joanna . . . we all have our part to play as we journey through life. Ask Jesus to show you what that is.'

The other children had been listening too and gathered round as Kelly-Ann sat at the piano and turned the pages of the hymn book until she found the one she wanted. She began to sing as she played and Joanna found herself singing too, then all the others joined in the chorus.

'This little light of mine, I'm gonna let it shine . . .'

It was a rousing chorus and everybody enjoyed singing it. It made Joanna feel a lot better.

'I suppose there'll be churches and choirs and Sunday schools in Singapore,' she said. 'And I can be part of them!'

The words of the last verse stayed in her head as she walked home.

'I took Jesus for my Saviour,
You take him too.
Let his light live on inside you
All your life through . . .'

Joanna felt such a very small light to be making such a journey. Everybody seemed to think it was a great adventure and said they envied her. But they're not the ones going! she thought.

Lunch was ready and she washed her hands and face before sitting at the table. Mrs Lacey said grace and served Joanna with vegetables.

'I had a word with Mr Coombes after church,' she said, starting on the potatoes. 'I explained that you won't be able to sing for him at Christmas.'

Joanna gulped and poured far too much gravy onto

her plate.

'He wonders if you'll help Stephanie to learn the solo part?'

Her appetite completely gone, Joanna fixed her eyes on her now tear-blurred plate and nodded. Since she was eight years old she had sung the solo, leading the choir down the aisle on Christmas Eve, allowed to stay up for the midnight service so that her pure treble voice could sing the first verse of 'Once in Royal David's City' and begin the celebration of Jesus' birth. In spite of all her resolve she just had to ask the question.

'Do we *have* to go before Christmas?'

'Yes, we do, Joanna,' Mrs Lacey sighed. 'And it's going to be wonderful . . . now eat your lunch!'

Cathy smiled as she smudged blue eyeshadow onto her left eyelid and squinted into the mirror.

'Do donkeys have blue eyes?' she wondered aloud.

'Ten minutes, everyone,' Mrs Boswell called from the classroom doorway.

Joanna tried to swallow the big lump that was blocking her throat.

'I think I've lost my voice!' she croaked, clutching at her neck with both hands.

'That's nerves,' Anne explained with her usual pursed lips and knowing expression. 'I feel terrible and I'm only a sheep! "We're shivering sheep – and it's too cold to sleep . . ."' she began, but stopped when the other sheep threw their woolly hats at her.

Joanna tied a silk girdle around the waist of her long blue gown and fastened the white head-dress with a hair grip.

'It's my last concert,' she told her reflection sadly.

Every year for as long as she could remember Joanna had taken part in concerts, nativity plays and pantomimes both at school and at church. She always had a special part to play and a song to sing by herself. She sang her first solo when she was three and surprised the audience with her ability to hold a tune, being so young. She even remembered the song:

'Jesus bids us shine with a pure clear light,
Like a little candle burning in the night.
In this world of darkness so we must shine,
You in your small corner, and I in mine.'

The words say just the same thing as the chorus we sang on Sunday, she thought. This little light of mine!

Everything seemed to be coming to an end. This was her goodbye performance at school, the packing cases were already in storage and the apartment bare. Mrs Lacey had collected the plane tickets and there were just five more days before the journey began. Joanna had been for a farewell tea at Anne's house and had spent the night with Cathy the weekend before. All her games, books and jigsaws had gone to the children's ward at the hospital and most of her winter clothes to the charity shop in the High Street. There was just one more school day left, for class parties and a final performance of 'Christmas Jazz' when the children from the infant department came to watch. Joanna felt that the time for last goodbyes was getting too close.

Then Mrs Boswell called, 'Time!' and Joanna found herself in the wings waiting for the music to cue the entrance of Joseph and Mary. She could hear Cathy singing her comical little song and peeped round the curtain to see her swing her rope tail. Joanna's throat was dry and there were at least six butterflies with very large wings flapping around under her sash!

Then she was on stage and the spotlight dazzled her so that she couldn't see the audience at all and she felt alone in the silence. For a moment her mind went blank then the music started and it all came back – just in time!

'My soul doth magnify the Lord . . .'

Joanna's voice was clear and true and it held the audience spellbound as the words of the Magnificat expressed Mary's joy at being chosen to be the mother of the Son of God. She sang so beautifully that when she had finished there was a long silence before the listeners burst into delighted applause.

Joanna, not sure whether her tears were happy or sad ones, took her bow and left the stage where Mrs Boswell, beaming all over her face, hugged her and Mr Brown patted her on the back saying 'Well done, Joanna!'

Joanna linked her arm through her mother's as they walked down the hill. It was a very clear night and quite cold with a million twinkling stars set in a black velvet sky.

'You were lovely tonight. I was so proud of you,' Mrs Lacey said, giving her daughter's arm a squeeze.

Joanna smiled and returned the squeeze. She liked the feeling when people clapped and enjoyed her singing. She liked the spotlight and being 'special' if only for a short time. She looked up at the stars. They shonefor a while and in the morning they were gone. The difference was that they would return to shine another night.

Mrs Lacey followed Joanna's gaze and smiled.

'The same stars shine in Singapore, Joanna,' she said.

'And you will be the same person. Nothing really changes — nothing that's really important. You are Joanna Lacey, wherever you are, and you can do whatever you want. It's up to you.'

Joanna nodded.

'I think I understand,' she said.

Joanna fastened her seat belt and held her breath until the aeroplane was high above the clouds and the red warning lights went out. The hostess smiled at her as she passed down the aisle with a tray of drinks for the passengers further up the cabin.

Mrs Lacey let her breath out in a long sigh that surprised Joanna.

'Were you scared too?' she asked.

'I always am — never did like taking off even though I flew lots of times before you were born. I'm fine now, though, and ready to enjoy it.'

'Were you scared when we went to Riyadh? I didn't notice.'

'You had your eyes shut, that's why!' Mrs Lacey laughed.

Heathrow had been a dismal place that morning. The sky was grey and heavy with what the weather report said would be snow before evening. Joanna had felt cold, damp and miserable as they had left Pavilion Mansions for the last time and the taxi had passed all the familiar places she felt she would never see again — the library, the park and the church with its tree-lined churchyard. Some of her treasured possessions were in storage, it was true, but she wouldn't be seeing them for a very long time and they felt 'lost'. Her hand luggage contained the few things her mother had let her bring.

'For,' she had said, 'no doubt you'll soon have a collection of new favourites!'

Joanna hadn't said, 'I prefer my old ones,' out loud, but she had thought the words inside her head.

'Two books and a treasure' had been her orders and the choice had been a difficult one. At last the big illustrated book of Bible stories had been safely stowed away after Joanna had promised to carry it all the way herself. Her second book choice was *The House at Pooh Corner* even though she could recite most of it almost word for word.

Once, not long after she had first learned to read and could manage some books with only a little help, she had mis-read a word and had Piglet heading for Eeyore's house in a high wind with his ears streaming out behind him like bananas! She was ten years old before she stopped reading 'bananas' and realised the word was 'banners'. How her mother had laughed and then bought her Piglet for her last birthday along with a pink beanbag for her bedroom.

The beanbag was gone but Piglet, resplendent in a freshly ironed T-shirt and his soft pink leather body carefully polished, was safely packed in her hand luggage. He lay between the two books and her chosen 'treasure' – the picture that Mr Brown had taken of the whole class in the play and presented to Joanna in front of the school on her last day. He had framed it for her in gold with unbreakable plastic instead of glass so that it would be safe on her long journey and Mr Brown had added his own special message . . .

*To Joanna, a prayer.*

Thank you Lord for all that makes me ME,

For making me unique.
Thank you for making me special to my parents
and friends and all who know me.
Help me to make the most of myself;
Help me to use my mind, my character,
my talents and my opportunities to the
very best advantage, always.

She understood what he meant. He was saying exactly what her mother had said the night of the play. She was still Joanna wherever she was, and she would always remember Mr Brown.

'It's going to be a long trip,' Mrs Lacey said, bringing her back to the present. 'How are you going to pass the time?'

Joanna grinned, diving into her bag and pulling out the pink stowaway much to her mother's surprise.

'I didn't know we had a fellow traveller,' she said, tweaking one of Piglet's 'banners'.

'He doesn't take up much room and he reminds me to look at everything carefully before jumping to the wrong conclusions!' she said, remembering the 'bananas'.

Mrs Lacey laughed then watched, puzzled, as Joanna took out a crochet hook and several little balls of coloured wool.

'What are you going to do with all that wool?' she asked, watching Joanna make a long chain out of a ball of bright yellow.

'It's a coat for Piglet . . . a coat of many colours like Joseph's . . . because he's going on a long journey to be a stranger in a strange land!'

'So are *we*,' Mrs Lacey pointed out.

'Yes, but I think we'd be stared at if we were wearing a many-coloured coat each. Piglet can wear his for both of us.'

'Like a representative?' Mrs Lacey asked.

With a nod of the head for answer Joanna frowned as she made the first double treble into the chain. The first one was always the hardest. Kelly-Ann had taught her to crochet and turn chains and trebles into little garments and table mats. She always had to concentrate on the first few stitches until she remembered *exactly* how Kelly-Ann had shown her, so talking was out of the question. Mrs Lacey settled down with her book and by the time the hostess arrived with a meal, the piece for the back of the coat was finished. For hours and hours that was all Joanna seemed to do – crochet a bit, sleep a little and eat a lot! Time meant nothing high above the clouds and it wasn't easy to remember what day it was with the time changing as they circled half the world. At last Piglet had his new coat and the plane made its final landing. The journey was over.

The heat and light were such a change from the grey English winter that Joanna gasped with surprise as they stepped from the plane. It was so *hot*!

An airport bus took them to the terminal building and Joanna could see real palm trees at the edge of the runway. Once out of the bus the heat hit them again and they hurried into the cool air-conditioned immigration lounge. There was a huge sign over the door which Joanna tried to read, to herself, for she didn't want to make a mistake pronouncing the words.

'Selamat Datang ke Singapura', a voice said.

Joanna turned round to find a very tall man in a purple turban smiling down at her.

'It means "Welcome to Singapore" and you say it just as it is written,' he went on.

Joanna thanked him and read the sign again, aloud. The man nodded as he moved away, giving her a wave as he disappeared into a rest room.

She held her mother's hand very tightly as they passed through endless barriers and had passports stamped and papers inspected. All kinds of people were talking in so many different languages that Joanna tried to shut her ears to all of them. She didn't like not knowing what people were saying!

'There he is!' Mrs Lacey cried, peering over the heads of the crowd.

Joanna couldn't see anything until they were clear of the barriers, then she felt the excitement too, for there was Daddy!

She recognised him at once even though he had grown a droopy moustache, like a Mexican cowboy, and his face and bare arms were a rich dark brown. How could she have thought she wouldn't know him?

'Daddy!' she squealed, running across the marble floor and into his outstretched arms. He swung her round and round until she thought her head would fall off and there were lots of hugs and kisses. Joanna thought she saw tears in her mother's eyes even though she was smiling.

'Here at last!' Mr Lacey said, as they scrambled into a waiting taxi that nosed its way into the stream of traffic outside the airport. 'I bet you have been counting the days, Joanna?'

She *was* happy to see Daddy . . . but how could she tell him that she wanted to stay at Pavilion Mansions and go to school with her friends? Joanna felt her mother's hand take hers and give it a reassuring squeeze.

'Yes, Daddy,' she said quietly.

# Chapter Four

The ride into the city was terrifying. The taxi dodged in and out of the traffic and the driver had his hand on the horn the whole time. All Joanna could see (when she dared to open her eyes) was a blur of bright colours, tall buildings and crowds of people rushing to and fro on what must have been very important business. Mr and Mrs Lacey talked all the way to the hotel and Joanna felt quite out of it, even though she was happy for her mother, whose eyes were shining.

The hotel was so high that Joanna had to lean backwards to see the top. The taxi-driver put his hand on her shoulder to steady her as she almost fell over.

'Take care, Missy,' he said.

*Missy*? What kind of name was that? Joanna pulled away, careful not to look at the man. Mr Lacey went to the desk to sort out their booking and they were soon riding in the lift to the twenty-second floor, where they stepped out onto thick carpets.

'A night of luxury living, then off to our own place!'

Mr Lacey said as he opened the door to the large airy room. It was a double room with a bed for Joanna tucked away in a corner. It had its own bathroom too.

'It's very cold in here,' Joanna said, surprised.

'That's the air-conditioning – you can turn it down if you like. The bathroom's through here.'

It was a very nice hotel room and the view from the big window was breathtaking. Twenty-two floors up, the room overlooked most of the area and there were many red-tiled roofs below her as Joanna looked down over the city.

'There's a swimming pool on that roof!' she exclaimed, pointing to another hotel further up the wide road that stretched to right and left.

'That's the Singapore Hilton,' Mr Lacey said. 'If you look around you'll see that many of the hotels have pools on the roof. The one here is on the ground floor, in the hotel garden.'

'What is this hotel called?' Joanna asked, trying to show an interest when really she felt quite dizzy perched up in the air like a bird.

'This is the Mandarin and it has thirty-six floors. Right at the top, making thirty-seven, is a restaurant that turns round and round so that you can look out over the whole city while you are eating!'

Joanna was sure that she didn't want to go any higher and left the window and the view.

It's just like any old city, she thought. All buildings and shopping and cars. What's so special about Singapore?

After a shower and a change of clothes Mr Lacey suggested they take their first real look at their new home.

'I'll get my coat,' Joanna said, moving to the

wardrobe.

'You won't need a coat here, Joanna – not even at midnight.'

'Then why did I bother to bring one?' she muttered under her breath, then bit her lip. Had anybody heard? Her father was busy counting the money in his wallet and her mother was adding lipstick to her newly made-up face. 'Thank goodness,' she sighed. 'Nobody heard!'

It was very hot, even for sandals and a cotton dress. The family strolled down Orchard Road on red-tiled walkways that were dotted with beautiful flowering trees, some with clusters of small pink blossoms and some with large white waxy-looking flowers but few leaves. Mr Lacey explained that Orchard Road was the main tourist area and it was full of splendid hotels and fantastic shops. They had ice-cold drinks at a pavement cafe called Ban Chuan and walked through several of the huge shopping complexes called plazas, each one four floors high and containing hundreds of shops. One of them, called Singapura Plaza, had an open area in the middle that was like a small park and glass see-through lifts that rose in full view up the four balconied floors. Joanna began to feel quite ill. One minute she was so hot she thought she'd melt, then the next she was shivering in the fierce air-conditioning that every store and complex had. It was all so bright and somehow disappointing. It was just like Harrods at Christmas. People were talking and shouting in words she didn't understand and then it grew suddenly dark and the lights were even brighter, shimmering in the tears that threatened to spill out and run down her cheeks any minute.

Joanna clung to her mother's hand as tightly as she could. All she could think of was that it was Christmas

Eve and she should be wrapping presents and building a snowman, not being pushed and jostled by people she didn't understand. As she thought again of the midnight service in her beautiful church, all lit up with candles, and the precious crib with the Holy Family that Kelly-Ann had made at pottery class, her tears rolled down and would not stop. Her mother excused her, hurrying her back to the hotel and bed, muttering about long journeys and over-excitement.

Joanna could see that her father was not pleased. He had wanted to show them everything and insisted that she would be fine on her own while he and Mummy went down for dinner. Her eyes closed and it wasn't long before she fell asleep even though it was the first time her mother had gone out without her.

There were presents on Christmas morning just like always – two very pretty cotton sun-dresses from Daddy, a pair of golden Indian sandals with a thong that went between her toes and a bright red personal stereo complete with headphones. Joanna had two presents for her parents in her bag – small ones because of the weight problem with hand luggage. Mrs Lacey loved the little heart-shaped locket that Joanna had saved so hard for and chosen with such care. Mr Lacey was delighted with his leather-bound address book and gave her a hug.

Joanna did try hard that first full day in Singapore. She had woken up some time during the night and had heard the murmur of voices from the other half of the room. She was sure it was Mummy telling Daddy how much school and her friends had meant to his daughter and cried a little, her head under the bedclothes to stifle the sound. Mummy was so happy with Daddy that it seemed mean to be miserable and spoil it for them.

They had Christmas dinner in the hotel, in the revolving restaurant on the thirty-seventh floor. Joanna had to admit that it was quite spectacular! The round dining room turned so slowly that you couldn't actually feel it going round, and the view was terrific. Facing south, Joanna could see Singapore River and the open sea and even bits of the island that weren't just like any other big city. She could see parks and gardens as well as skyscrapers and traffic-blocked roads.

'Why isn't everybody at home for Christmas?' she asked.

Mr Lacey smiled. 'Look around you,' he said. 'All these people come from many different cultures. The Chinese only stop working on their New Year and the Hindus and Sikhs celebrate Divali . . . their festival of light. You'll see many festivals, Joanna, and they're all different.'

Joanna looked down at her plate. The turkey had tasted like turkey and there was even a coin or two in the plum pudding. Every place had a cracker beside it and the bangs could be heard at the end of each course.

'Isn't this wonderful, Joanna?' her mother said, putting on the paper hat from inside her cracker.

Joanna smiled and nodded and kept her mouth in its fixed grin for the next few minutes. How could it be wonderful? It was too hot to be Christmas and people should be at home with their families, not pulling crackers in a roundabout restaurant! There should be chestnuts on the fire and all the Christmas TV like Disneytime and Scrooge. How could Christmas in a posh hotel be wonderful?

All Joanna's good intentions disappeared and her

mouth quivered and turned down at the edges. A terrible feeling began low in her stomach and started to rise to her throat.

'It's not wonderful at all. It's horrid and I hate . . .' and with that she ran from the table hesitating at the lift only until she remembered it had an attendant.

Mr Lacey found her sitting on the floor in the corridor outside their room, her knees up under her chin and her back against the locked door. She was crying quietly into a large white handkerchief thoughtfully provided by an American gentleman from the next room.

'I'm sorry, Daddy. I'll try, I really will,' she sobbed as Mr Lacey unlocked the door and led her into the room.

'Tell me all about it, Joanna,' he said.

She tried – but her father didn't try to understand at all. He just went on and on about what a lovely place it was and how happy she would be sooner than she knew and what an awfully cold and miserable place England was. He didn't seem in the least interested that she had left all her friends and all the things that were important to her.

They moved to the air base that afternoon. Mr Lacey had been given married quarters for himself and his family and he was anxious to get them settled. The move made things even less like Christmas.

The base was on the northern tip of the island, away from the smart city and the shops. The taxi chugged along a narrow road between thick greenery that Joanna was sure was jungle. There wasn't a sign of human life anywhere and she kept getting bitten by tiny flies that caused itchy lumps. The quarters were separated from the main buildings by the airfield and a golf course and looked like a village of white bungalows each with its own little garden. Their bungalow was a square squat building quite a way back from the narrow metalled road. It had a steep, red-tiled roof and there was a huge tree at the front. Inside it was bare except for very plain tables and chairs and the beds were just old-fashioned mattresses on spring bases.

'I'll get new beds when we are settled,' Mr Lacey promised. It was very hot inside until he found the switches that turned the great flat-bladed fans that hung from the ceiling. 'That's better,' he said with a smile.

Mrs Lacey pulled a face at Joanna then smiled too. Joanna didn't smile back. She couldn't believe that her father meant them to live in this horrid place!

'Mops and buckets I think,' Mrs Lacey said, still smiling as she pretended to roll up her sleeves ready for some hard work.

'There isn't any glass in the windows!' Joanna observed.

'Who needs glass?' her father grinned. 'It's never cold and the shutters will keep out the rain – when it rains.'

The bungalow had a large living room with a dining table at one end and a cane suite with faded pink cushions. A rickety old coffee table with black metal legs completed the furniture and the whole lot stood on a grey tiled floor. A fair sized kitchen at the back, with a cooker and an old-fashioned fridge, opened onto a covered walkway that led to a small outbuilding. From the main room a long dark corridor led to the bathroom, toilet and two bedrooms. There were no windows in the corridor and it was very dark. Joanna went into the toilet and turned on the light.

Her shriek brought both her parents to the rescue. The floor and walls of the small room were covered in huge cockroaches with shiny brown backs, all scrambling to escape the light.

'Always remember to turn on the light and wait two minutes before you open the door,' Mr Lacey said without much concern.

Joanna shuddered and went into the small room that was to be hers. It was situated right at the end of the building and had windows in two of its walls. The floor was bare, a cool covering of marble tiles that looked fairly clean. A plain wooden dressing table and a wardrobe that didn't even match were the only furnishings except for the narrow bed with its rusty looking springs. She pushed the shutters open and looked out at the back of the house. The ground sloped away to another line of bungalows at the bottom of a piece of waste land with a path running through it. There wasn't a garden but at the end of the flat bit, that she supposed was theirs, there was a line of weird-looking plants that made a sort of hedge. Her eyes widened as she peered at the bunches of bananas that hung from the leafy fronds.

'Ears like bananas!' she whispered to Piglet, hugging him, then sitting him against the mirror on the dressing table. The sound of excited voices drew her back to the window to see four or five sun-tanned children, boys and girls, running along the path in t-shirts and shorts.

'Hang on, Philip,' one of the girls called. 'I feel a bit crook!'

Joanna couldn't imagine what the girl meant but she recognised the accent from the Australian films she'd seen on television. The figures disappeared behind the banana trees and Joanna turned back to her room. It didn't take long to make it more homely. The brown paper packages and the string-tied bundles that were piled on the kitchen units proved to be things that her mother had asked for on the telephone while they were still in England. Joanna's bed soon had pretty pink sheets and pillowcases on it. There wasn't a duvet though, for as Daddy said, 'Who needs a duvet in this heat?'

A silky white Indian rug filled the narrow space between her bed and the dressing table and a round basket chair gave Piglet a more comfortable perch. Mr Lacey left them to their cleaning and walked down to the village, returning in a taxi with a box of groceries, a cooked chicken for tea, a brass lamp with a pink shade for Joanna's room and a pair of white elephant bookends for her dresser. They looked a bit silly with just two books between them so she decided to use them as ornaments and keep the books on the chair by her bed until her library grew again.

Nobody had called her for the evening meal. She sat on the edge of the bed feeling very lonely and left out. They had always done things together, she and Mummy. Now Mummy had Daddy to talk to and Joanna was alone.

She pulled her big book onto her lap and searched through the well thumbed pages. There were so many lovely pictures and there was usually one that could make her feel better. She paused at a page that often made her feel sad. Jesus, all alone in the wilderness, and a few pages along Jesus alone again, in the garden of Gethsemane. She sighed. Jesus was not afraid of being alone because God was with him.

'God was with him,' she whispered, looking round the little room she had tried so hard to make like home. God is everywhere, she thought, closing the book and kneeling beside her bed.

'Lord Jesus, be with me in this strange land and help me to be loving and kind, and most of all, unselfish.'

She sat on her bed again and opened her bag, taking out the photograph that had been her parting gift from Mr Brown. There she was in her blue dress. It brought back such happy memories that she began to sing Mary's song, softly at first, just to herself, then as the music filled her she let the song ring out and held the last 'amen' until she had no breath left.

There was no burst of applause or pat on the back. The faces of Anne and Cathy grinned at her from the picture. There they were, together, and they would forget she ever existed! Then, as though she were not miserable enough, she felt a sharp sting on her ankle. Looking down, she screamed at the sight of a hoard of huge black ants crawling across her toes and a red swelling where one had taken a taste of her flesh. She leapt onto the bed and put her hand on the wall to steady herself – and then screamed even louder as a six-inch lizard, who had been sitting there minding his own business, ran over her hand in his eagerness to escape the giant that was attacking him.

At that moment a brilliant flash of lightning and a huge crash of thunder shook the building and torrential rain beat on the roof and bounced on the dry ground outside.

'*I hate this place!*' Joanna screamed at her mother when the door opened. '*I hate everything!*'

# Chapter Five

Joanna opened the shutters and looked at the bright morning. Beyond the bungalows at the bottom of the slope was an open area, grassy and with clumps of trees.

'It looks like a park!' she said with some surprise. She had expected palm trees and these looked just like the trees in the churchyard at home. She swallowed hard.

'Stop it!' she told herself. After last night she had better try to hide her feelings, she decided.

A bright yellow bird flashed through the banana trees and perched, singing a series of warbling notes, before he tore long strips off the wide green leaves. There was no sign of yesterday's storm. The earth was dry and parched-looking and the sky was blue and cloudless.

It only took a minute to put on a T-shirt and shorts and slip her feet into sandals then, washed, brushed and with clean teeth, she made her way along the corridor, past the master bedroom and out through the double doors onto the front verandah. A long stretch of flat-bladed grass ended at the roadway and opposite was another bungalow just like theirs, and another and another, all exactly the same.

'It looks just like Anne's estate,' Joanna said quietly.

She walked across the strange-looking grass, watching carefully for anything that crawled or slithered, and stopped at the big tree that marked the corner of the garden. A huge spider had spun his web between a branch and the bushes at the side. Joanna quite liked spiders. Of all the creepy things spiders were the least horrid. The tree trunk divided into two above her head and there were nobbly bits to make climbing easy. Once settled comfortably in the fork, she had a good look at her surroundings. There were many bungalows either side of the stretch of road, each one with a patio at the front, full of potted plants and climbing greenery. The only colour other than green was supplied by the bushes that separated each property. They had large red flowers dotted about them. Above her the branches of her own tree, although almost bare of leaves, had tulip-shaped red flowers hanging from every twig.

About six bungalows along, the road turned a corner and rose steeply, turning left and ending in a clump of tall palm trees almost black against the sky. She heard voices and saw two figures walking towards her from the direction of the gates and the airfield. Joanna could see that they were both dressed in lengths of patterned cotton tucked in round the waist and falling almost to the floor. Both ladies were wearing sandals and brightly coloured T-shirts and their many bracelets jangled and glinted in the sun. One of them called a greeting as she passed by but Joanna was too shy to answer, not understanding the words.

A rumble inside her reminded her that supper had been a sandwich in her bedroom the evening before and she was glad when her mother appeared on the verandah and waved.

'You're an early bird, Joanna,' Mrs Lacey called. 'Come and have breakfast!'

Joanna climbed down and walked slowly across the grass to join her mother.

'It's very quiet,' she said.

Mrs Lacey put an arm round Joanna's shoulders.

'Quieter than last night?'

Joanna looked at the tiled floor.

'I'm sorry, Mummy. I didn't mean what I said.'

Mrs Lacey gave her a squeeze and Joanna sighed. Her mother *always* understood.

Mr Lacey was eating breakfast and looked up as the pair joined him.

'Good morning, Daddy,' Joanna said, slipping into the chair opposite him and pouring herself some juice.

Mr Lacey finished his piece of toast and washed it down with the last of his coffee.

'Who's this?' he asked. 'Not that awful girl we met last night!'

Joanna bit her lip. She didn't know what to say except 'sorry' but she felt a little better when her father ruffled her hair as he left the table.

After breakfast, when Mr Lacey had gone to work across the airfield, Joanna and her mother went shopping. It was quite a walk to the store with its NAAFI sign over the door and they were both hot and uncomfortable as they entered the air-conditioned building.

'What does NAAFI mean?' Joanna asked.

'Navy, Army and Air Force Institute,' her mother said.

'We should be able to get everything we need here.'

It was a big store, like a supermarket, and all the usual English things were on the shelves like baked beans and brown sauce. There was a clothing and footwear section and a whole room full of electrical goods. By the cash-out desk was a news-stand and Mrs Lacey bought a *Singapore Times* and a *Bunty* magazine for Joanna, putting in an order for it to be delivered every week.

'Isn't this weather lovely?' she said as they walked home with the heavy carrier bags.

Joanna didn't answer. She could feel her arms stinging as the sun burned her fair skin and she was glad to get back into the bungalow and turn on the fans. How boring it was! There was nothing to do and nobody to be with, not even a television to keep her company. The cane chairs were not very comfortable and flying things kept buzzing past her ears. How could *anybody* think that *this* was lovely!

She was half way through her *Bunty* when she heard the voices. Three ladies, one of them very large, were standing at the patio doors looking at her.

'Is your Mom in, sweetie?'

Joanna jumped to her feet and ran to call her mother who was just finishing a cool shower, refusing to go back into the room until they went together. Mrs Lacey called, 'I won't be a minute,' and dressed very quickly.

'You are a silly,' she whispered as they hurried along the corridor.

'I don't know them,' Joanna explained.

'Neither do I – but we can still be polite!'

Joanna sat down with a bump and buried her nose in her magazine, hiding her face with her long hair. Who are these people? she thought grumpily.

'Welcome to the base – I'm Janice Kelly, no relation to Ned, and this is my neighbour, Sam Howlett.'

'Short for Samantha,' a very thin lady with bleached hair added, crossing the room to sit on the settee.

'And I'm Mary Creasey,' the third visitor said, holding out her hand.

Mrs Lacey shook hands with each one and they were soon chatting over a pot of coffee and a plate of biscuits. Joanna grunted an answer once or twice when she was included in the conversation. They had never had visitors at Pavilion Mansions. She had been looking forward to spending the rest of the morning alone with her mother, as they always did during school holidays, and now it was all spoilt.

Suddenly she realised that everyone was looking at her and her mother's eyebrows were raised.

Had she been asked a question?

'Joanna!' Mrs Lacey's voice rose to match her eyebrows and Joanna jumped to her feet.

'I was just suggesting that you go out and find the other kids,' Mrs Kelly said. 'They're all having a great time out there. Why don't you go and find my Philip?'

Her mother's face said *go* and she did just that, screwing her eyes up against the glare. There didn't seem to be anyone about but rather than go back inside she walked to the big tree and leaned against it.

Joanna felt very lonely. Her father was angry and her mother was busy with her new friends. She hadn't met *this* feeling before – the one that made her purse her lips and resent other people taking her mother's attention. Usually, when things were not right, she would read one of the stories in her book and that would make her feel better but she couldn't even do that because she'd have to pass those people to get to her room.

Suddenly, with a whooping and a great deal of laughter, a group of boys and girls on bicycles came screeching down the hill and round the corner, only stopping at Joanna's tree . . . one of them even running into it with a front wheel.

'G'day . . . You new?' said a dark-haired boy on a racing bike.

'Who are you?' asked a small girl with freckles on her face and arms, pushing her nose right up to Joanna's when she didn't answer the boy.

'Cat got your tongue?' another boy said, throwing his scrambler bike onto the grass and approaching the tree with his hands on his hips.

'I'm Joanna Lacey.'

'She's a *Pom!* A *Brit!* Look at her white pommy skin and yeller hair! Is your name Snow White . . . *Pom?*'

Joanna couldn't believe her ears. How rude they all were!

'Mind your own business!' she snapped.

'Ooh . . . listen to her!' the dark boy said. 'Mind your own business!' He spoke in a silly voice and stuck his nose in the air. 'Don't be so stuck up, Pommy!' he finished.

That started all of them and they danced round Joanna and her tree pulling faces and chanting *'Pom Pommy Pom!'*

Joanna could feel her face going red, she was so angry, and without thinking of the consequences she launched herself at the horrid boy, hitting and kicking and crying all at the same time. Mrs Lacey ran out of the house to see what all the commotion was about and the three visitors were close behind.

'Philip! Are you hurt?' Mrs Kelly shrieked, catching hold of his arm and turning him to see if he was.

Mrs Lacey hurried Joanna inside, mouthing apologies and saying goodbyes as the children climbed on their bikes and scattered.

'Whatever were you doing?' she said as they made for the bathroom.

'He called me a *Pom!*'

'That doesn't mean you have to hit him, Joanna. I don't know what's got into you. I've never known you to fight like that.'

'I never have,' wailed Joanna, wincing as a sticking plaster was pressed onto her cut knee.

They went into the kitchen together to make lunch, being very careful not to spill anything on the floor to attract the ants that could detect a grain of sugar at fifty yards.

'I know it's all strange and very different, Joanna,' her mother said, as she washed a lettuce she had bought that morning. 'It is for me too! But I think I'm going to enjoy living here. At least I'm going to give it a try, when I've got used to the heat, and the creepy-crawlies . . . and the insects that bite . . . and . . .'

'And lizards?' Joanna added, trying to smile through her tears.

'Are those real tears . . . or are you peeling onions?' Mrs Lacey asked.

'I love you, Mummy,' Joanna said.

'And I love you too!'

Mr Lacey arrived for lunch, riding an ancient bike with squeaky wheels. Joanna heard him first as he turned off the road and braked as he crossed the grass.

'I'll get you a bicycle, Joanna. It's quite safe to ride

on the base and all the Australian kids have them. Have you made any friends yet? No? . . . Oh well, it's early days!'

Joanna was glad her mother didn't tell him about the fight. She was sure he would be angry because he wasn't as patient with her as Mummy was and wouldn't wait for her to explain. After the light lunch she went to her room because she could see that her parents wanted to talk to each other and she felt in the way. When Mr Lacey rode off on his bike again her mother came to find her.

'Daddy says there's a swimming club on the base, at an open air pool, and it's this afternoon. Let's go and sign you up!'

Joanna was sure it was going to be awful as they set off with their swimsuits under their shorts and tops. Everything else was! She was hot and sticky even before they reached the end of their little road. The married quarters were separate from the main base so unless they went out of one gate, along the main road and in at the other gate (where they had to show a pass) they had to cross the airfield by a little path that ran alongside the runways where there was no shelter at all. The sun beat down and made Joanna's head ache and she nearly jumped out of her skin when a noisy jet flew low overhead and landed on the other side of the airfield.

'I think we'll have to get you a sun hat, Joanna. Your nose is going red already!'

A *sun hat?* That would really make them call her names!

Joanna put her hand over her nose to shield it from the sun until they were through an archway and into the pool area. It was lovely. The water was very blue and there were shower stands at both ends. At the side a stretch of normal looking grass was dotted with tables, each with its own umbrella, and a little café was selling Cola and crisps. A few children were already in the water as well as some toddlers who were splashing in a learner pool at the bottom end. Joanna began to feel a little better until a lady with a very red face approached them, waving a piece of paper.

'No public swimming . . . it's Aussie club day. I'm afraid it's members only.'

Joanna heard her mother explain who they were and that they'd like to join, then couldn't believe her ears when the lady said, 'I don't think we can accept Singaporean Service children!'

Joanna felt her face going red again. 'I'm English!' she said in a loud voice.

'Yes . . . but your Daddy is with Singapore Air Force, dear, and if we let you in . . . well . . . who knows what it might lead to? It is the Australian club day and we do have our rules!'

Joanna walked away and stared down into the water. It looked so cool and she was so hot.

'Bet you can't even swim!' a voice at her elbow jeered. It was that horrid Philip again. He yelled as Joanna pushed him in and stayed under for quite a while, spluttering to the surface and glaring at her.

Mrs Lacey looked quite angry herself as they walked home, and suggested that Joanna had a rest in her room after the ordeal. She lay on her bed with the fan turning slowly overhead and let her mind go back to England. She went all the way through bonfire night and the play and remembered one or two adventures she'd had with

Anne and Cathy. It made her very sad to remember all those happy times. She'd never hit anybody then, or pushed them into swimming pools.

'It's this place that's changing me,' she decided.

The photograph of the class was on her dressing table and she leaned over to get it, sitting up and turning it over to read the message on the back.

'Thank you for making me special to my parents, my friends and all who know me,' she read. The trouble was she didn't know anybody and she didn't have any friends. She wasn't sure that her parents were too happy with her either. 'It's so hard to be *me*,' she said.

Mr Lacey arrived home at six and by half past it was dark. It was still hot and the fans had to go on whirring away all the time they were having tea. Lizards ran up and down the walls but, as her father ignored them, Joanna supposed it was usual. Their voices were almost drowned out by the noisy crickets and frogs and Joanna said that it all sounded like the noises on films about jungles. Mr Lacey reminded her that the jungle wasn't very far away. After the dishes were washed and put away and every scrap of waste collected and put in the bin outside, Joanna suggested a game of some kind to pass away the evening.

'We have a lot of catching up to do, Joanna, Mummy and I, and I've invited some people round for drinks. Haven't you a book to read or something?'

'We'll get a television from the NAAFI tomorrow,' Mrs Lacey promised. 'One of those little portable ones. Then you can watch it in your bedroom.'

Joanna kissed them both and went to bed. There didn't seem anything else to do. She heard the visitors arrive and she was called out in her pyjamas to meet them but as soon as they had said hello they turned away and talked to each other and there was a lot of laughing going on. Several ideas entered her head. She could pretend she was very ill and needed a cooler climate. Who would believe that? She could be so awful that Daddy would send her back to live with Cathy. That was even more stupid!

There wasn't anything to do but grin and bear it.

## Chapter Six

'Our first Sunday!' Mrs Lacey said, piling her long blond hair on top of her head in a knot.

Joanna smiled. Her mother always looked nice but today she looked especially nice. Her face was golden brown and she didn't need any make-up, except for a dab of pink lipstick. Her face was all shiny and young-looking. The sleeveless dresses she wore suited her slim shape and yesterday, at the NAAFI, the manager had thought they were sisters instead of mother and daughter. Mrs Lacey had blushed and Joanna had never seen her do that before.

Wearing a pink sun-dress and her Indian sandals, Joanna walked to the base church at the gate. She could see it was meant to be a church, because it had a large cross on the gable end, but the building itself looked like the old scout hut on the edge of her junior school playground back in England. It was a prefabricated building with a rubber tiled floor and window panes of frosted bathroom glass. A table with a white cloth stood at the end opposite the door and the pews were just rows and rows of ugly orange plastic chairs. Joanna remembered her beautiful St Mark's church at home and felt very sad. She sang the hymns as best she could to the out-of-tune piano, her voice making everybody turn round to see who was singing so nicely. The vicar gave his sermon; which was not really a sermon but more of a story.

Perhaps it's because there are a lot of children, Joanna thought. The story was one that Joanna knew well. Kelly-Ann had told it to her Sunday school class and they had all found the Bible reference and printed it alongside their drawings.

'Luke chapter ten, verses twenty-five to thirty-seven,' the Vicar began. . . . then he told the story in his own words. He told how on one occasion when Jesus was preaching to a large crowd, a young lawyer who thought he could trick Jesus, stood up and asked, 'What must I do to be sure of eternal life?'

'What does the law tell you and what have you learned from your reading?' Jesus asked.

The young man replied, 'It is written that I must love God with all my heart, with all my soul and with all my strength. And I must love my neighbour as much as I love myself.'

'That's right,' said Jesus. 'If you follow those rules, you can be sure of eternal life.'

But the man asked another question . . . 'Who *is* my neighbour?' And Jesus answered him with a story.

'A man was travelling along the road from Jerusalem to Jericho when he was attacked by thieves who beat him, took all his money and left him lying wounded in the road. A priest came along and when he saw the man he crossed to the other side of the road. Some time afterwards one of the Temple assistants came along and when he saw the injured man he passed by too. Then a third man came along, a stranger, a Samaritan. When he saw the man he stopped to help him, washed his wounds with the oil and wine that he was carrying and bandaged them. Then he lifted the man onto his own animal and took him to a nearby inn. He gave the innkeeper some money for the man's keep until he was well and promised to pay any extra when he passed that way again.

Then Jesus turned to the young lawyer and said, 'Which of these three was neighbour to the man who was attacked?'

'Why, the one who looked after him of course,' said the lawyer.

'Then go and do the same,' Jesus said.

The last hymn was one of her favourites . . . 'When I needed a neighbour were you there?' and then the service was over.

'That's one of the stories Kelly-Ann told us at Sunday school,' Joanna said to her mother on the way out of the building.

'Yes, and it says a lot too, doesn't it? That we should be kind and loving to all people all the time,' her mother answered.

Joanna felt ashamed. She hadn't been kind to *any* of the people she'd met and she'd been rude to most of them!

As they shook hands with the vicar at the church door he said, 'That's a very nice voice you have there, young lady. I hope we can count on you for a solo now and then?'

Joanna stood to one side as her father introduced her and her mother to Padre James, as the vicar was known. The sky was overcast so it wasn't too hot. She had enjoyed the singing and the story had reminded her that Jesus wanted people to be kind and loving to each other but just as she was promising to try, a voice behind her made her angry again.

'Pommy show-off!'

It was that horrid boy Philip and Joanna forgot about being like the Samaritan and pulled a face at him.

At that moment the sky burst open and rain poured down, straight down and so hard that Joanna could hardly find a spare bit of air to breathe. Nobody seemed to mind it much and the congregation plodded across the airfield getting wetter every second. Joanna found it quite delightful because the rain was warm like a shower and by the time they reached Meteor Road, where their house was, she was paddling ankle deep. It stopped as suddenly as it began and the sun came out, drying everything in minutes and by the time they reached number twenty-four her clothes, the grass and her hair were quite dry.

The Christmas and New Year celebrations came to an end and it was time to start thinking about school. Joanna avoided all contact with the Australian children, preferring her own company and a full colour book about the island that her father had borrowed from a friend at work. The thought of being in a classroom with Philip and his friends filled her with dread. She was learning a lot from the book. Why couldn't she go on learning by herself? She knew now that the red flowering bushes at the side of the garden were hibiscus; that the waxy white flowers in Orchard Road were growing on oleander trees and that her own perch was in a tulip tree. The local name for the greyish/pink house lizards was chit-chat and the gardener who came to cut the grass was called a kabun and his name was Sammy. Awas meant danger and aedes was the Malay word for the malaria mosquitoes. She'd learned that from an insect spray advertisement in the local newspaper. As it turned out, she wasn't even allowed to attend the Australian school and that made her mad. Who did they think they were? It was humiliating! She could see Philip Kelly through a classroom window and he mouthed 'Pom!' at her. She made a face and turned away. Who wanted to go to their stupid school anyway?

It was a nice building though, with a gym and everything. The alternative was the local government school in Bukit Merah, a biggish village four miles away.

Bukit meant hill and merah was the colour red so the sign on the front of the grey bus really meant Redhill Village and the road 'Jalan Bukit Merah' was really Redhill Road.

The school looked awful. The buildings were low and had corrugated iron roofs. Hundreds and hundreds of children were running about, all wearing uniforms, the girls in old-fashioned green gymslips and the boys in white shorts and shirts.

Joanna's was the only blond head among the dark ones and she was stared at like a freak! Things went so fast and she met so many teachers, prefects and girls that she was very confused as they left the grounds. Under her arm was a brown paper parcel containing the dreadful uniform and a letter of permission to start school the next day.

'Do I have to go to school?' she asked. 'Couldn't you teach me at home, Mummy?'

Mrs Lacey shook her head. 'We all have to learn to be part of where we are, Joanna. Besides, I'm an English teacher for seniors. I'm not sure what you should be learning!'

Joanna sighed. It seemed that *her* feelings never mattered at all! The afternoon wasn't all bad, though, for Mrs Lacey decided that they should explore the village while they were there and for the first time Joanna began to enjoy herself.

The village was one long main street of shops, all open to the pavement, with baskets of funny-looking fruits and dried fish. Eggs, covered in a layer of black mud, were labelled as being one hundred years old and Joanna wrinkled her nose at the thought of the smell.

I suppose they're just old and bad, Joanna thought. Coloured awnings and blinds gave shade as they walked and the shopkeepers were only too pleased to let 'Mem' and 'Missy' try slices of chilled fruit. Joanna liked rambutan best, twisting the spiky red cases to reveal the white ping-pong ball sized fruit, sweet and juicy. Huge mangoes and papaya and watery star-fruit were all tried and Mrs Lacey bought quite a lot.

A flower seller was offering bunches of real orchids, all colours and very exotic for only two dollars.

'That's only fifty pence!' Joanna said, knowing that there were four Singapore dollars to the pound.

There were clothes shops and general stores like *The Chinese Emporium* where you could buy almost anything! Mrs Lacey spent a long time browsing among the bottles and jars in a chinese medicine shop and bought a little red tin of Tiger Balm ointment, world famous and good for all ills. There was a history leaflet with it about the Haw brothers who had invented it and a list of all the things it was said to cure.

They found a market with livestock: chickens, ducks and a litter of little pink piglets that Joanna wouldn't look at because she had a feeling they were going to be somebody's dinner very soon!

In an open paved area at the end of the village they found an eating house with stalls under umbrellas. Mrs Lacey had a coffee and Joanna had a Coke. All around were local men with cages, each with a small bird inside. One by one the cages were hoisted up a high pole and, once at the top, the little bird sang and sang. It was a competition and the man that won received a fancy golden trophy. He gave his bird a handful of seeds and stroked its brown and yellow head.

The cafe owner set in front of Joanna a little dish of very thin noodles covered in a brown sauce. He grinned and waved his hands to say 'no' when Mrs Lacey offered to pay.

'For little missy to try,' he said.

Joanna had a taste and gasped, grabbing her drink and finishing it in one go. It was *hot!*

'What is it?' she cried, fanning her mouth with her hand.

'Mee Siam, Missy, Mee Siam . . . Very good! Yes?'

Joanna ate it all, with the help of a glass of water to cool her, and enjoyed it when she got used to the tingling in her mouth.

As they walked back to the bus stop near the school Joanna felt very differently about Singapore. This was more like she had imagined; old buildings, chinese hats and funny food; people in saris and samfoos – the blue blouson and black silky trousers that she knew the name of from the time they did Aladdin at school. Everyone was smiling and friendly and that made her smile too.

They were laden with baggage as they trudged home; bags full of exotic fruits, a bunch of purple orchids, two lengths of paisley patterned cotton so that they could wear sarongs in the house, several pairs of sandals because they were so cheap at three dollars a pair and Joanna's school uniform still in its brown wrapper. It had been a lovely day, just Joanna and her mother, like it used to be.

Mr Lacey was waiting on the patio with a jug of cold pineapple juice.

'Where have you two been?' he asked. 'I've been home ages and ages!' He ruffled Joanna's hair. 'Go and see what's in your bedroom,' he said to her. 'A better-late-than-never Christmas present.'

A little red television set was on her dressing table, with a triangle of metal tubing for an aerial and a very good picture of Scooby-Dooby-Doo in magnificent colour on the screen.

Joanna ran back into the lounge and flung herself at her father who picked her up and danced about the room.

'There's someone out there!' she gasped as they passed the window and she saw the light in the out-building.

'So there is,' Mr Lacey said. 'It's your amah in her amah's quarters.'

'My what?'

'Your amah, your nursemaid, mother's help, servant. Her name is Jaya and she's from the village.'

'I don't need a nursemaid,' Joanna said, feeling very

uneasy.

'We can't leave you on your own at night, can we?' Mr Lacey went on. 'That wouldn't do at all.'

Joanna looked at her mother who was trying on a pair of green sandals.

'We have to go out sometimes, Joanna,' she said without looking at her daughter. 'We've had lots of invitations. All the other children have amahs.'

Joanna didn't feel quite the same as the other children.

'Can't I go too?'

'They're grown up evenings, I'm afraid . . . but you'll be fine with Jaya and your TV.'

It was a nice little television and there were lots of English programmes on Channel Five as well as Chinese and Indian films with sub-titles, the sort she'd seen at home now and then. The Malaysian channel seemed to show cartoons most of the time and she enjoyed '*Upstairs, Downstairs*' which she had heard her mother talk about but had never seen.

Something outside screeched and it made her heart beat very fast. She sat up in bed and held her breath. What was it?

There! The noise happened again and Joanna was really scared. The shutters at the back window were still open and she crept across the tiny room to close them. She had just fastened the little brass bolt when the loudest screech of all startled her so much that *she* screamed even louder and knocked over the basket chair in her haste to get back into bed.

'If I'm eaten alive it will be Daddy's fault,' she whimpered to Piglet. 'Mummy never left me when we lived in England, just the two of us.'

How she wished it was still just the two of them . . . in the flat at Pavilion Mansions where things didn't screech in the dark!

'It's not fair,' she said to a passing chit-chat. 'I haven't any friends and I'm left all alone and told to "Go and play" or "Go and read a book!" *It's not fair!*'

'Missy?'

There was a knock on the door and it opened just a crack. A brown nose and one eye appeared then a slim figure with a long glossy plait of hair stood in the doorway.

'Something wrong Missy?'

Joanna didn't know what to say. How was she supposed to talk to an amah?

'I heard a funny noise,' she said, feeling a little foolish.

The girl crossed the room and opened the shutters, peering out into the darkness.

'It is nothing – just a night bird. He is gone now.'

Joanna got out of bed, turned off the TV and followed the amah into the living room.

'Can I have a drink?' she asked.

'Of course, Missy.'

Joanna liked being waited on. She found that the amah did everything she said . . . 'Fetch my sandals . . . get me another drink'. It was just like *Upstairs, Downstairs*.

'What's your name?' she asked, forgetting what her father had said it was.

'Jaya is the name to call me – my real name is very long.'

'What is it when it's long?' Joanna asked, beginning to like the Indian girl who had come to live with them.

'Jaylahmenatullah. . . . my father's name is Saddhakhatullah.'

'I think I like Jaya and it's easier to say!' Joanna said. 'Will you play Scrabble with me?'

Jaya didn't seem to mind how late Joanna stayed up and they played Scrabble and Snap and watched an Indian film that made Jaya cry. Joanna loved it when Jaya sang along with the girl on the film, even though she didn't know what it was all about. When the amah went to her room to get a handkerchief Joanna went too and was surprised to see how nice the little outbuilding was. It was like a doll's house, or a Wendy house for playing in. Jaya was very happy to be living there with a room of her very own and had added many of her own possessions to make it homely. She told Joanna that it was the first time she would sleep in a bed, for at her own home the family slept on the floor on rush mats.

On a little table under the window was a picture of a strange creature with many arms and a woman's face. Candles and flower heads surrounded it and a garland of whitish-yellow flowers with tiny petals hung from the top corner of the frame.

'What's that?' Joanna asked.

'It is a shrine,' Jaya explained, 'where I pray.'

Joanna was eager to hear all that Jaya could tell her and sat on the bed to listen.

'This is the goddess Parvati. She is the goddess of loving kindness and peace. Sometimes she is called Kali and then she is fierce like a warrior. I pray to her when she is Parvati, the wife of the god Shiva.'

'But there is only *one* God,' Joanna said, her eyes wide with amazement.

'That is true,' Jaya went on, 'but he has many faces.

Brahman is the One Great Power that is in everyone and is everywhere all the time. Our smaller gods each show one aspect of Brahman – one of his many faces. Do you know the story of the blind men and the elephant?'

Joanna shook her head.

'Hindus do not say theirs is the only correct religion,' Jaya explained. 'We say that all religions are a search for truth. People may call the truth by different names but this does not change what it is. Once long ago five blind men were told that they were to meet an elephant, a creature none of them had met before. Each man was able to reach only a part of it. One who touched the leg said an elephant was like a tree and the one who touched an ear described a fan. Another, as he held the tail, said that an elephant was like a snake . . . and so on. Each man thought that the bit he felt was the whole elephant. Each one had part of the truth but none understood it completely. Hindus say there are many ways of looking at the truth and that there are many paths to the top of a mountain. Once at the top does it matter which path has been taken?'

Joanna didn't answer straight away and as Jaya had found her handkerchief the pair set off back to the main house. Once there the amah disappeared into the kitchen to make a chocolate drink and Joanna ran to her bedroom to get her picture Bible. On the last page was a very special picture, showing Jesus ascending to heaven in a shaft of golden light, and underneath it were the words she had been trying to remember.

'Go out into the world and tell the good news to everyone. Find new followers in every country and teach them what I have taught you, and know that I shall be with you always, to the end of time.'

'I liked your story,' she said as Jaya came into the room with two mugs. 'Come and look at my book.'

The two sat on the settee and looked at the picture Bible. Jaya thought the pictures were beautiful and knew all the stories as well as Joanna did, which surprised her!

'We studied Christianity at school,' Jaya said, 'at Bukit Merah.'

'That's where I'm going tomorrow!' Joanna cried.

'You'll like it there,' Jaya went on, sipping her drink and nodding her head.

When Mr and Mrs Lacey returned from their night out they found two girls asleep on the settee; one dark and one fair and across their knees was an open book, open at a picture of Jesus, his arms wide open to receive all people.

# Chapter Seven

Joanna stood at the school gates.

'I don't want to go to this school,' she mumbled, pulling at the collar of her school blouse and hating the green tie she had to wear with it. Her feet were hot and uncomfortable in socks and gymshoes and she envied her mother with bare toes and a sun-dress.

A group of small children ran past, pointing and giggling and one of them, a small boy, ran up to her and said, 'Hello, girl with the golden hair . . . Give me some golden hair and I am very rich!'

The other children shrieked with laughter and Joanna felt very angry and miserable, both at the same time.

The walk up the drive was quite an ordeal with all the eyes watching her and then her mother spoke to Mr Toh, the headmaster, and kissed her on the cheek.

'Mr Toh will find someone to show you round and he will see you get the right bus home. Do your best, Joanna.'

Watching her mother walk down the driveway was terrible to Joanna. How can she leave me here she thought, with all these people that I don't know? Doesn't she care about me any more?

The headmaster told her to sit on a wooden bench by the verandah rail. The verandah ran all the way round the square of buildings and was open to the central yard. In the middle of the yard stood a tall flag-pole and hundreds of children were standing in lines around it.

'I have to take assembly,' Mr Toh said. 'You can take the test afterwards. Please wait here.'

Joanna felt sick inside. A test! Why did she need a test? She had been near the top of the class all the way through junior school and Mr Brown was always saying how pleased he was with her progress. Why did she have to take a test?

The assembly began with the raising of a flag to the top of the flag-pole, then the whole school sang the Singapore national anthem. Joanna recognised it from the television and it began 'Mari kita rakyat Singapura.' She hadn't managed to catch the rest of it. Mr Toh started to talk to the rows of pupils standing to attention in the hot sun, shouting a lot and flinging his arms in the air. As he walked back towards the verandah and his office, music blared out from loudspeakers positioned at the bottom of the pole and the whole assembly started doing exercises, bending knees, touching toes and swinging arms to right and left.

I'll never do that, Joanna thought fiercely. I don't care who says I have to!

A Chinese secretary came out of the school office and presented her with a pile of papers and a blunt pencil while a tall boy with a knot of hair on top of his head placed a folding desk in front of her. Mr Toh appeared again and spoke to his secretary before approaching Joanna.

'Please do all you can. Take your time; someone will come in a while.'

The children filed out of the courtyard and into the rooms that opened onto it on all four sides. Joanna was left alone on the verandah outside the office. She looked at the first paper. Mathematics! She wrote her name at the top, left the bit where it said 'Grade' empty and stared at question one.

'Get on, please . . . don't sit staring!' said a small Chinese lady who hurried past without even looking at Joanna.

She looked at the paper again.

1. How many mangoes at fifty cents each can you buy for three dollars?

2. $(4+8+6) \times 2 = \ldots$?

Joanna frowned. This was the sort of work she had done in infant school. It was much too easy for her! She looked at the second sheet.

1. Place an adjective before the noun in each sentence.

a) The girl wore a. . . . dress.

A bell rang, echoing round the buildings, and immediately the courtyard filled with boys and girls who surged across it and down the verandah past Joanna. Everybody stared at her and pointed and one little girl actually touched her hair!

'Tie back the hair, please!' a teacher said, handing her a black shoe-lace.

How awful I must look, Joanna thought, pulling her

hair into a tight pony tail at the back of her head. She could feel her eyes filling with tears and brushed them away with the back of her hand.

'Get on! Get on, you lazy girl!' another tall teacher snapped.

Joanna put the pencil down very slowly. She certainly wasn't lazy! She was still sitting there with her arms folded when a boy collected her papers and a girl rang the big handbell again.

It was break. Groups of children were sitting on the paved yard and eating rice out of plastic lunch boxes with their fingers. The girl who had rung the bell asked Joanna to go with her for the break period.

'Mr Toh says I must look you,' she said. Then when Joanna looked puzzled she continued, 'Come, please, to canteen for break. I bring you here again.'

The canteen was just a huge corrugated tin roof supported on four poles. At one side was a square of counters with a sort of kitchen in the middle. Cooks in white smocks stirred and mixed and served out little bowls of thin noodles and bigger bowls containing something that looked a bit like rice pudding.

'You want buy?' her guide asked.

Joanna had a dollar note in her pocket, safe inside a real leather purse that Jaya had given her. She knew she needed twenty cents for the bus home so that left eighty. She could see a list of prices hanging from one of the poles . . . mostly ten or twenty cents an item.

'Mee Siam?' she asked, her voice a tiny squeak.

'You know food names?' the girl beamed, collecting a little bowl and paying ten cents for Joanna. 'No, you buy tomorrow,' she said.

The bowl of noodles was hot but not as hot as the

one she had tasted with her mother at the little café in the village, and Alice, her friendly guide, bought a tin cup of orange for her that was really good. There were so many questions that Joanna couldn't answer. She knew that the Chinese, Indian and Malay students were all speaking English to her but she only understood the words like 'name' and 'house'. She managed to give her name and where she lived but explaining what she was doing in a government school was too much for her audience. She was glad when the bell went again for it was very hot and there weren't any fans. The children were all saying her name and touching her — her hair, her arms and her cheeks. 'Yowhan' they seemed to be calling her instead of 'Joanna', and Alice told her it was the tiny golden hairs on her arms that the children were interested in, for they didn't have any.

They think I'm a freak in a circus! Joanna thought.

They didn't go back inside but had to line up in the courtyard. She couldn't see what was happening until she got to the front of the line. Everybody was drinking from tin cups and when she tasted hers she spluttered and wiped her mouth with her hand.

'It's horrid,' she said.

'You drink it, please,' a tall boy said, making sure Joanna saw his prefect badge.

'No, thank you. I don't like it,' Joanna said, holding out the cup.

There was a lot of shouting and pointing and no-one was speaking English any more. Joanna didn't know what was happening except that a fierce-looking teacher with a turban and a black beard was shouting at her. Mr Toh appeared and explained that everybody had to drink the soya bean milk to be sure they had plenty of protein and vitamins.

'It is for good health,' he said. Joanna tried to say that she was sure her mother gave her the right things to eat but it didn't make any difference. She drank the milk and everybody laughed at the face she pulled.

Then came the very worst thing. Everybody marched down to the deep culvert, the monsoon drain, that ran the length of the drive and crouched over it, brushing their teeth with worn toothbrushes taken from a pot of salt. A mouthful of water from a ladle dipped in a white plastic bucket, was poured into their mouths and a rinse and a spit in the drain completed the exercise. Joanna refused.

They all stared at her as she stood outside Mr Toh's office. Some were laughing but others looked scared and Joanna wondered if they used the cane in Singapore! The thought made her legs shake and she had to clench her fists and bite her lip to keep from crying. She heard the telephone 'ping' as Mr Toh picked it up and the 'whirr' it made as he dialled a number.

'Hello . . . Mrs Lacey?'

Joanna gulped. He was calling her mother. Nobody had called her mother from school, not ever!

'Well . . . I don't *care!*' she muttered. 'I hate them all.'

By the time Mr Toh said 'Come in, please', Joanna had stopped feeling miserable and felt very angry instead.

Mr Toh didn't shout like the other teachers.

'I have spoken to your mother,' he said quietly. 'We are agreed that you may eat and drink what you choose but cleanliness is important. Teeth must be cleaned after food and drink . . . but you may bring a small bag for your own brush and toothpaste.'

Joanna sighed with relief. Mother wasn't too angry and understood.

Mr Toh's next sentence made her heart sink again though.

'You do not seem to know very much so I will put you with class 3B. Then we can see how you manage and perhaps move you when we know you and your work better.'

Joanna couldn't believe it. She knew that Singapore primary schools were for children from six to twelve and that classes were named 'standards'. There were six standards, and Bukit Merah school had so many children that there were four classes in each standard. Being put in Standard 3B meant she would be with children of eight and nine who were not the best students – and she would be *eleven* at Easter!

'But I'm in the top . . .' she began but Mr Toh held up his hand for silence.

'We will see how you progress,' he said. Then he added kindly, 'Perhaps – in time.'

Mr Toh dismissed her into Alice's care. She took her to the classroom and there Joanna sat, staring at the board and doing as little as possible of the simple mathematics until it was time to go home.

Each morning Joanna caught the bus to school and sat at her desk. The work given her took a very short time and she spent most of the school day gazing out of the windows. Each afternoon she arrived home at two o'clock to find the house empty but for Jaya. Mrs Lacey had made many friends, played tennis on the courts behind the Officers' Mess, had learned to play golf and was much sought after for coffee and a chat. When she asked Joanna how it was at school the answer would be 'Fine, Mummy,' and that was that.

'You're always out!' Joanna complained one tea-time.

'I was always out at home too, wasn't I?' Mrs Lacey reminded her. 'But then I was working. Now I'm enjoying myself.'

I'm not! thought Joanna.

Jaya still played board games and helped her with jigsaws but Bible stories and Indian goddesses were not mentioned again. Joanna was so unhappy that even her big book was left on the basket chair unread.

There was *one* happy thing. A Malay girl who lived in the bungalow at the bottom of the slope behind the banana plants went to Bukit Merah school too and travelled on the same bus. The day they met was an awful day. Joanna had been humiliated even further by being sent to Standard One to learn Mandarin from the beginning. Her own class were too far ahead for her to catch up. Joanna argued that she didn't need to learn the official Chinese language but as always nobody listened and she had to go. Everyone passing the windows could see her sitting with the littlest ones and had grinned at her. Joanna was sure they were laughing at her and had rushed out when the break bell went to get as far away from the six-year-olds as possible before the rest of the classes were dismissed. In her hurry she didn't look where she was going and ran straight into the slim figure on the verandah steps. The apologies had set them off talking and now they were firm friends.

Aniki's father was a major in the Malaysian Air Force, spending five years in Singapore training young pilots. The family – Aniki's mother, father and three little brothers – came from Ipoh, a biggish town in the northern part of Malaysia. That first day, travelling home together on the bus, Joanna had told her new friend how awful the day had been and how much she hated school. Aniki knew exactly how Joanna felt.

'When I first came from Ipoh,' she said, 'I found everything very strange, too. In my last school lessons were told to me in Malay and the English I learn as a second language. Here the lessons are told in English, all except Chinese Mandarin, and I know nothing. I was in a low class until I learned better the English.'

Since that day the two girls had travelled to school and back again on the same bus and met in the canteen at break. Joanna spent some evenings at Aniki's house and often had tea there on Jaya's day off. The little brothers, Rafel, Mandhir and Chiram, were full of tricks and made Joanna laugh with their antics. Sometimes Aniki cooked for them both, strange noodle dishes and coconut sweets that melted in the mouth. Joanna thought the whole family were very good-looking. Aniki's father was tall with jet black curly hair and a moustache a bit like her own father's. Mrs Chandar was tiny and round with a face that was always smiling. She didn't speak any English at all but smiled and nodded and nodded and smiled whenever Joanna caught her eye. The little boys – twins who were five and the baby, Chiram – were chubby little bundles with black eyes and very white teeth. Joanna could never tell Mandhir and Rafel apart. Aniki was very pretty with lots of dark curly hair which twisted into tiny ringlets on her shoulders. She kept it partly covered at school with a thin chiffon scarf and wore tight-fitting trousers of white cotton under her uniform. At home she always wore coloured trousers and a loose long-sleeved top that fell to her hips. Aniki had real gold studs in her ears and

Joanna had never seen such beautiful teeth, and as Aniki was always smiling her teeth were always on show.

One tea-time Rafel's new kitten purred around Joanna's legs and rubbed its body on her ankle. It was a pretty black and white kitten and Joanna bent down to stroke it, running her hand along its arching back and all the way to the tip of its tail.

'His little tail has a bend in it!' she exclaimed. 'It's bent right at the tip with a nobbly lump . . . Has he been in an accident?'

'No accident,' Aniki laughed. 'All small cats have the tail broken when they are born. . . . just as dogs have a little snip from one ear.'

It seemed, to Joanna, a very silly thing to do. 'How cruel,' she said, picking up the kitten and cuddling it under her chin. 'Why would anyone want to do that?'

'Only Allah is perfect . . . and man in his image,' Aniki explained. 'Animals cannot be perfect.'

The very next Sunday Joanna decided she was not feeling too well and asked to be excused church. Mr and Mrs Lacey set off across the airfield and Joanna could see they were holding hands. She felt very left out and not part of a family any more.

'I wish I was Aniki,' she told her reflection in the dressing-table mirror. There were so many brown spots on the mirror that she looked as if she had the measles. 'And I wish I had *real* measles,' she went on. 'Then I wouldn't have to go to school tomorrow!'

'It's all so confusing!' she said to Piglet who was still wearing his many coloured coat. Joanna could hardly see him through her tears. She remembered how Piglet was to be a 'representative' for herself and her mother, wearing the rainbow colours to cheer them up when it wasn't possible to dress that way themselves. 'Mummy has forgotten all that,' she said sadly.

Slowly Joanna removed the crocheted coat. All that was past, all gone. Piglet was just a leather toy to remind her of *The House at Pooh Corner*, and that was past too. She didn't feel like remembering things.

Kelly-Ann and Sunday school were so far away and she didn't feel able to talk to Jesus, not even a little bit. It was all so confusing. Jaya had her statue of Parvati and Aniki had a kitten with a bent tail.

'What does it all *mean?*' Joanna asked.

# Chapter Eight

The next Tuesday, when Joanna had been in school nearly two whole weeks, she arrived home to find Jaya out and Mrs Lacey cooking lunch. Aniki hadn't appeared at school so Joanna had spent her breaktime alone but for a crowd of little boys and girls who wanted to touch her fair skin, and she had sat by herself on the bus.

Bacon, eggs and fried tomatoes was such a change from chicken, rice and egg noodles that for once she smiled.

'That looks good!' she said. 'Is it English bacon?'

'Danish!' her mother answered. 'I went to the city this morning with Mrs Kelly and there, in Fitzpatrick's, down Orchard Road, I saw *bacon!* And how about *these?*'

All Joanna's taste buds sprang into action.

'Crisps!' she sighed, rolling her eyes and pretending to faint into a chair. Crisps like the ones sold in England couldn't be bought anywhere near the base . . . even at the NAAFI!

'After lunch,' Mrs Lacey said, placing a full plate in front of Joanna, 'we'll have a long lazy afternoon together.'

'Isn't Daddy coming home for lunch?'

Mrs Lacey shook her head.

'He's on a training flight over Malaysia, all the way up to Butterworth and out over Penang Island. He may be back tonight, or maybe not.'

Joanna wriggled with delight. A whole afternoon and perhaps the night . . . Just the two of them, like it used to be.

'We haven't spent much time together, have we?' Mrs Lacey began, as she sat facing Joanna with coffee and some toast. 'We'll have to have a long. . . .'

'Halloo! Anybody there?' a loud voice called from the patio. It was the red-faced lady from the swimming club, waving a piece of paper with a lot of noise and bustle as she came into the room. 'Oh, sorry . . . I didn't think you would be eating at this time of the day!'

Joanna looked at the clock. It was two-thirty.

I suppose they get home from school earlier than me, she thought. But they don't have to take a horrid bus full of horrid people!

The afternoon was already spoiled and she could feel her mouth turning down in an ugly sulk.

'I've got the forms,' the visitor went on. 'It took a great deal of talking and explaining but you're in.'

Joanna knew what she meant but kept her face as blank as possible. It was the membership of the swimming club.

'How lovely,' Mrs Lacey said, smiling as she took the form and read it. 'We can go this afternoon, Joanna.'

'I shouldn't swim after a meal,' Joanna said quite

sharply.

'The walk across the airfield will soon shake that down! We start at three,' the club secretary said, as she heaved herself out of the chair and left through the patio doors.

Joanna closed the door of her room and leaned against it. She remembered the last visit to the pool and how she had pushed the hated Philip in at the deep end. Her new swimsuit was hanging in the wardrobe, still in its clear plastic packet. Joanna took it out and held it in front of her. The swimsuit had been chosen in happier times, its rainbow stripes attracting her then. Now it just looked gaudy and childish. They were sure to laugh at her.

'There are no rainbows here,' she said to Piglet.

For the first time in what seemed like ages but could only have been days, Joanna sat on her bed and took the big picture Bible from her basket chair. The promise God made to Noah stretched across a double page . . . a perfect arch of colours over the Ark perched on Mount Ararat. She could hear Kelly-Ann's voice telling the story of the forty days and forty nights of rain that killed every living thing except those who were in the Ark with Noah . . . two of every kind. All the Sunday school class had crayoned a rainbow and sung 'The animals went in two by two'. Joanna had been seven then, and the rainbow was very special. Mummy had bought rainbow socks and motifs to sew on her jumpers and God's promise that everything would turn out fine had made rainy days bearable.

'Come on, Joanna. It will be over before you get there,' her mother called.

She closed the book with a thud and left it on the

bed.

The pool was quite full. Good swimmers were doing back crawl widths at the deep end, while another crowd were kicking their legs and hanging onto white float boards in the shallows. Joanna could see Philip Kelly and his friends diving in the top corner as she walked with her mother to the group of parents gathered by the baby pool.

'Hello. So glad you've come!' the club secretary called, ushering them into the centre of the circle.

Joanna didn't pay much attention to what was being said because that horrid boy was pulling faces at her from the water and all his friends were giggling at something he was saying.

'Joanna!'

Her mother and the secretary were looking at her, expecting an answer of some sort but luckily, before the silence became uncomfortable, the young woman at the poolside called her to join the beginner group.

'Off you go,' Mrs Lacey said with a smile. 'Enjoy yourself . . . I'll pop off and do some window-shopping in Orchard Road. We were just organising getting you home. Philip's mother will give you a lift so you won't have to walk after your swim. See you at tea-time.'

Joanna couldn't believe it. The afternoon was supposed to be a 'together' time and there was her mother strolling off to window-shop, a thing they always did together, and leaving her with strangers and people she didn't like!

'Can you swim?' the young coach asked, leading Joanna to the shallow end.

'Of course I can. I'm not a baby!'

'Really? Then you'd better dive in and prove it. We

don't want to put you in the wrong group, do we?' the coach said sarcastically.

Joanna gulped. She didn't swim all that well. One lesson a week for one term at school in England had not made her an Olympic swimmer and she wished she had not answered so readily.

'I can't dive very well,' she said. 'Can I get in the water first?'

She edged her way down the side of the pool until she came to the steps, and walking down them she was very much aware that everybody had stopped swimming to watch her.

Red-faced, and really rather scared, Joanna set off across the pool, her clumsy breast-stroke causing a great deal of splashing. She managed it, though – all the way across, hitting her head on the side rail and finally opening her eyes as she stood up. Then she heard it.

Philip and his pals were sitting on the side, laughing and pulling faces and pointing at her. One of them dropped into the water and splashed across the pool. She knew the girl was mocking her and just couldn't bear it a moment longer. The steps were quite near and Joanna scrambled up them before running along the side of the pool. Philip and two other boys fell into the water with shrieks and yells as her well-placed foot tipped all three of them into the pool. Joanna heard their yells and their parents shouting as she made for the archway and the path home. She had grabbed her sandals and towel bag from one of the tables as she ran and her feet were burning as she hopped from one to the other on the hot path. Her hair had dried by the time she reached the end of the airfield and she could feel it sticking to her face in untidy strands.

Once near the married quarters she stopped, pulling her shorts and t-shirt over her sun-dried swimsuit and wriggling her toes into her sandals. The path back to the pool was empty and Joanna sighed.

'Phew. . . . I bet I'm in trouble now!'

'Trouble?' a voice said right behind her. 'What has happened?'

It was Aniki, crossing the grass from the direction of the NAAFI. It didn't take long for the story to be told. Joanna walked with her Malay friend as far as the gate. Aniki explained that the bag she was carrying contained food for her grandmother.

'She lives in a kampong and is very old. I go to see her every week and take nice things for her to eat. A kampong is a clearing in the jungle . . . with houses.'

'Why does your grandmother live in Singapore when you come from Malaysia?' Joanna asked.

'It was all called Malaya once. Singapore was part of it. The grandmother was born right here in Kampong Bungar. It is my father's mother. My father left to live with relatives in Ipoh when he was a little boy and it was there he married my mother.'

They had reached the gates and Joanna looked up and down the main road.

'Can I come with you?' she asked.

Aniki grinned.

'I would like that,' she said. 'And grandmother would too, but should we ask your mother?'

Joanna shrugged her shoulders.

'I can do what I like,' she announced. 'Nobody minds much. My mother's gone shopping and won't be back for hours.'

'Tell Jaya then, I'll wait here for you,' Aniki suggested.

'I don't have to tell Jaya where I am. Besides, I'm supposed to be swimming until five o'clock. We'll be back before I'm even missed.'

Joanna knew that what she was doing was wrong. She had never gone anywhere without her mother knowing exactly where she was and who she was with. It was an exciting feeling and she felt thoroughly naughty.

Nobody will ever know, she told herself, trying to ignore the little voice inside her that reminded her that God knows everything that people do. For a moment she did hesitate, then grabbed Aniki's hand.

'Come on,' she urged. 'I'm dying to see a kampong.'

The path wound its way through bamboo groves and trees that were thick with hanging vines and creepers. Plants with huge flat leaves filled both sides of the narrow track and Joanna stayed very close to Aniki. She was afraid she might lose the path and be lost. The jungle was full of noise: twitterings and clickings and the whirring of insect wings. It was hot but the sun could hardly get through the greenery overhead so it was not too unpleasant. They seemed to walk miles before Aniki said, 'Here we are,' and the path opened onto a clearing. Joanna thought she had never seen anything quite so lovely.

The smooth sandy floor of the clearing looked as if it had been swept and brushed into an even circle and round the edges five houses stood on brick pillars. Each one had a carved gable and shutters and decorative open-work on the wooden walls. A few chickens strutted in the darkness under the houses and a pair of goats munched young bamboo shoots beside the biggest house. In the centre of the clearing was a small mound, like half an igloo built from red bricks.

'What's that?' Joanna asked.

'The kampong well. I'll show you later,' Aniki promised.

The grandmother was sitting in a large cane chair and beamed when Aniki arrived. Joanna couldn't see very much at all. It was quite dim inside the stilt-house and it took a few minutes for her eyes to adjust after the glare of the sun in the clearing.

'This is Joanna, Grandmother,' Aniki said. 'She is the English girl I told you about.'

The old lady held up her cheek for a kiss, then Aniki put all the packets and tins she had brought into a kitchen cupboard by the side wall. There was quite a lot of conversation between Aniki and her grandmother but as it was all in Malay, Joanna couldn't understand any of it.

'I am to make tea for us all,' Aniki said by way of explanation and led her friend into the kitchen. It was very light in the little room at the back of the house, mainly because there weren't any walls! A corrugated iron roof on top of four poles had been added to the one-roomed house and under it was a Calor-gas stove and various cupboards and tables. A large plastic bin with a tightly fitting lid held water and Aniki took some to fill the kettle, using a huge enamelled ladle.

'The water is low, Grandmother!' she called. 'I'll fill up again before I go.'

When the tea was made, the two girls sat on the polished wooden floor sipping the hot liquid.

'I've brought coffee and tea, rice and salt and a big packet of egg noddles,' Aniki said to Joanna, blowing her tea to cool it before speaking to her grandmother again in Malay.

Joanna looked at the room. The stilt house had only the one room but it was quite large. It had a raised platform at one end, just to the left of the door to the kitchen. On the platform were several rolled up pieces of matting. Joanna counted them. There were seven. Apart from Grandmother's chair, the kitchen cabinet, a small table and two dining chairs the room was empty.

'There are seven mats!' Joanna said as she finished her tea.

Aniki nodded. 'They are sleeping mats and there are seven people in the house. Two aunties, three cousins and a cousin's wife. They all work in Jurong.'

'Jurong?'

'There are many factories in Jurong. The cousins who are married are saving up to buy a one-roomed flat there. They have booked for the eighteenth floor when the new block is finished.'

Joanna couldn't decide which she would prefer; a flat up in the air with a toilet and a bathroom or a home like this – clean, airy and right in the middle of a jungly garden.

The grandmother spoke to Aniki in Malay then turned to Joanna.

'You like live Singapore?' she asked.

Joanna nodded and whispered, 'Yes'. How could she tell the sweet old lady that she hated it? There were nice bits, like today with Aniki, and the day in the village with her mother had been lovely, but that had only happened once. There were more awful bits than nice ones and she swallowed the lump in her throat as she thought of the swimming pool and what she had done that afternoon.

Aniki moved the tea mugs and fetched two plastic buckets from the kitchen.

'Will you help me fill the water barrel?' she asked, her white teeth all showing as she grinned.

Joanna followed her to the red brick igloo in the clearing and was amazed to discover it was the entrance to a tunnel. There were twelve steps down, and they were well worn with the hundreds of pairs of feet that had tramped up and down them. Once at the bottom Joanna's eyes were wide with amazement. She stood in a cave-like vault, the roof held up by brickwork, and in front of her a round pool held icy cold water. A rocky path led round one side of the pool and a clear spring ran from a crevice a foot above the water.

'Oh, how lovely,' Joanna cried, clasping her hands together in delight. Shafts of sunlight filtered down through cracks in the roof over the stairs and these sparkled on the water, sending dappled light on the walls and the ceiling. 'How absolutely fantastic!'

Aniki giggled.

'You would not say that if you had to take a bath in there,' she said. 'It is very cold!'

Aniki explained that the kampong people washed their clothes – and themselves – in the pool. Drinking water came only from the spring above the pool. Joanna felt very peaceful in the cave well. It almost felt like being in church. It was sort of comforting. Memories of home and her own church came flooding back and for a moment she was going to ask Jesus to help her be the old Joanna, but she didn't.

He doesn't care about me, she thought.

By the time the water was poured into the barrel and goodbyes had been said, it was quite late. Aniki held

Joanna's hand as they made their way along the paths to the road. Joanna was quite scared and was glad that Aniki knew the way so well.

The sun had gone when they reached the bungalows and the short twilight between day and night was almost over.

Joanna took a deep breath and walked in through the open patio doors. Mrs Lacey was on the telephone and Joanna only caught two words – 'I'm frantic' – before her mother turned and saw her. 'Where on earth have you been? I've been out of mind with worry!' she cried, rushing over and pulling Joanna close.

Joanna couldn't speak. Not only did she not know what to say to her mother but she could see her father coming across the grass from Aniki's house with a very angry face. He was home!

'Go to your room!' he said.

Joanna hurried down the corridor and into her little bedroom, very unhappily, for she knew her father was right behind.

'What were you thinking of, Joanna?' he stormed. 'We couldn't think where you could be. Didn't you realise how worried we would be?'

Joanna stared at the floor.

'Have you *nothing* to say?'

Taking a deep breath as she decided what to say Joanna sat down heavily on her bed.

'I didn't think . . .' she began.

'That's *exactly* it!' her father interrupted. 'You just didn't think at all. How could you be so selfish as to hurt . . .' and so he went on and on while Joanna clenched her lip between her teeth to stop herself shouting out. At last she couldn't help it and with her fingers in her ears she stood up and shouted:

'I didn't think anyone would *care!*'

There was silence. Mrs Lacey opened the door and joined the pair who were glaring at each other across the room.

'What did you say, Joanna?' she asked, calmly and quietly.

'Who cares where I go or what I do?' Joanna wailed, sitting down again and staring at the floor.

'I care . . . and Daddy cares. Whatever do you mean?'

Joanna gulped. Now she had started she was going to have to finish it, and it wasn't easy.

'Nobody cared when I didn't want to come here, nobody listened to what I wanted. I wanted to stay where I was happy. I loved the flat and I liked my school and my friends. I was *somebody* there. I was special. I thought I was special to Mummy because we did things together and we were friends and I thought I was special to God because I can sing . . . and I hate it here and I hate school and you leave me out of things and leave me with Jaya and you go out and have parties and I . . . I . . .' she stopped, wiping the tears from her cheeks with Piglet who she had picked up without realising it.

Mr and Mrs Lacey each put an arm round Joanna as they sat either side of her on the bed.

'What was the word you used most of all, just then?' her mother asked.

Joanna thought.

'I,' she said, her voice hardly more than a whisper.

'I think we'd all better have a talk,' Mr Lacey began, 'because I think we've all been thinking of ourselves and what we want. I'll begin. I've always lived in hotels and barracks and I *did* mind when Mummy wanted to stay in England with you after you were born. I felt lonely and left out and sometimes angry when my friends had their families with them. Now I can see that I have wanted Mummy all to myself and that was selfish . . . I'm sorry.'

Mrs Lacey gave Joanna a squeeze.

'I'm sorry too. I was so excited at being here, and being on holiday instead of teaching. I forgot to make sure that you were happy. I've been thinking of myself, too,' she said.

Joanna blew her nose on the tissue her mother gave her and sat up straight.

'I'm sorry I went with Aniki without telling you,' she said, 'but I really didn't think you'd mind where I was.'

'I mind a great deal, Joanna, and so does Daddy. You are very special to both of us. Why didn't you say how unhappy you were?'

Joanna shook her head from side to side.

'I didn't think it would have made any difference. I asked Jesus to let me stay in England and that didn't make any difference either!'

'I'm sure Jesus listened to you, Joanna . . . but sometimes his answer isn't what we want to hear! I think we have all been a little lost, don't you?' Mrs Lacey asked.

Joanna nodded her head.

'Once, when there was a big argument between two of the boys in my class Mr Brown sorted everything out. He said it was "all a matter of communication" and that people don't talk to each other enough. John and Michael stood at the front of the class and told each other how they felt. It was so funny because the quarrel was really over something silly and we laughed. John and Michael were friends after that. I really liked Mr

Brown,' she ended with a sigh.

'Mr Brown was right,' Mr Lacey said. 'We have to get to the bottom of our problems with each other and talking things out can do that. The hard thing is to sort out the problems inside us and that's where talking things out with Jesus is so important.'

Joanna nodded again.

'I haven't talked to him for a long time,' she said ruefully. 'I was so silly to forget that he cares.'

Mrs Lacey leaned over and took the picture Bible from the chair. She turned the pages very slowly until she found the place she wanted.

'Look,' she said. 'Jesus tells us that even the hairs on our heads are numbered. Of course he cares.'

Joanna spent the next half hour telling her parents exactly what had made her so unhappy and very soon nothing seemed so terrible after all. She found that she did miss her English school and her friends but liked Aniki and Singapore quite a lot too.

'Let's make lists,' her father said. 'Good things and bad things!'

They all went into the living room and sat at the table with sheets of paper and pencils. The table was soon covered with thoughts and ideas until the results looked like three shopping lists.

'The good things can look after themselves. Let's look at the "Don't like" lists,' Mr Lacey suggested.

It took a long time. Each item was carefully read and discussed.

'You go out with friends and leave me with Jaya,' was one.

Joanna was forced to admit that sometimes the nights with Jaya had been very enjoyable and that she wouldn't have liked the grown-up parties very much at all. Her parents admitted that they hadn't taken *her* anywhere much . . . and they all agreed that perhaps *that* was the trouble! The quarrel with Philip was really silly because Joanna hadn't tried to be friends at all and she was reminded how she had disliked Anne at infant school because she was always showing off in front of the teachers. It had been a birthday party at Cathy's that had changed Anne into a friend.

The subject of school was the next on the list.

'I'm in the wrong class,' she had written.

'Whatever are they thinking of?' her mother cried. 'I'll ring the headmaster first thing in the . . .'

Joanna stopped her to admit that she had made a mess of the test on purpose and that it was not the school's fault.

'Why didn't you tell me?' her mother asked.

Joanna didn't want to say 'I didn't think you cared' again because by now she was realising how silly she had been. She didn't have to say anything because two arms gathered her close and gave her a hug.

'I think that we have all been a little selfish, don't you?' her mother asked.

Mr Lacey agreed and joined in the hug, much to the amusement of Jaya who came in at that moment and was surprised to see them all tangled up together.

'No cooking tonight, Jaya,' Mr Lacey said with a smile. 'Go and get ready. We are all going out for dinner!'

Joanna put on her pink sun-dress and the golden sandals she had hardly worn. She brushed her hair thoroughly until it shone and smiled at herself in the mirror. It's a much nicer face when it smiles! she thought. Then, while she waited for everyone else to get ready she knelt by the side of her bed and closed her eyes.

'Dear Jesus,' she began. 'I have been very silly and selfish for weeks and weeks and I am very sorry that I haven't been to church or said my prayers. I was so busy grumbling about what I wanted that I didn't think about anybody else at all. Please help me to understand that Mummy and Daddy want to be together on their own sometimes and that because they love each other it doesn't mean that they love me any less. Help me to be friends with Philip and to make things right at school . . . and forgive me for being horrid.'

'Come on, Joanna, I'm starving!' Mr Lacey called from the hallway.

'Just coming!' Joanna replied, then, 'Thank you for my Mummy and Daddy and thank you for loving me even though my light wasn't shining very much for a while.'

Joanna skipped along the corridor for her evening out, a tune humming inside her head . . . 'This little light of mine . . .'

# Chapter Nine

Joanna sat next to the window so that she could show Aniki the restaurant as the bus passed by.

'There it is!' she cried, pointing out of the glassless window. 'That's the table we sat at, right there under the tree.'

Aniki craned her neck to see and nodded.

'I can see it,' she said. 'I've never eaten there, though.'

Joanna settled back into her seat and sighed. It had been such a lovely evening.

They had arrived at the restaurant at eight o'clock when it was almost empty. Mr Lacey explained that most people ate out much later, sometimes even at midnight! It was very warm but a little breeze rustled through the big tree they sat under and the fairy-lights swung to and fro, making coloured ripples over everybody. Mr Lacey ordered several dishes from the menu, while Jaya and Joanna had large glasses of Cola filled with crushed ice. When the food arrived Joanna didn't know what to think and was just about to wrinkle her nose when a little voice inside her said, 'You don't know until you try!'

She was presented with chopsticks and there was a lot of laughter as they all tried to eat with them. Joanna gave up and used a spoon. She tried a sweet and sour grouper fish first and although it looked very ugly it tasted delicious and the dish of chicken and cashew nuts in an oyster sauce was fantastic! A tasty dish of fried rice and thin slices of pork with pink edges was her favourite, though, and she ate and ate until she could eat no more.

'A toast,' Mr Lacey said, raising his glass and standing up. Joanna giggled and stood up too, holding her glass of icy Cola high in the air.

'To the Laceys,' he said. 'And Jaya – and a new beginning.'

'Here we are,' Aniki cried, struggling out of the narrow seat and putting her school bag on her shoulder. 'Wake up!'

'I'm not asleep,' Joanna grinned. 'I was just daydreaming.'

Once inside, Joanna went straight to the office and handed in the letter her mother had written that morning, then made her way to the courtyard for assembly. She found she knew most of the national anthem just by hearing it every morning and for the first time she joined in, singing what she knew as well as she could. At the end of assembly a young Chinese teacher whom she didn't know asked her name.

'You have a very nice voice,' she went on. 'I would like to hear you again some time.'

One or two of the girls in the line were nodding and smiling and Joanna smiled back.

'Why aren't you in the choir?' a tall Indian girl asked

as her line moved off. 'Talk to you later . . .'

At the end of the first lesson Joanna was sent for and she stood outside Mr Toh's office feeling far from brave. He was sure to think her very stupid. Once inside she relaxed because he was very understanding.

'It must be very difficult to leave all you know and love behind you . . . I don't think I would have liked it, Joanna. I have lived here all my life, went to this school as a boy and still have my childhood friends all around me. I do wish you had said how you felt though!'

'Can I take the tests again?' Joanna asked.

'Certainly, and I think you will find they get harder and harder on each page. It is a way of discovering just what a student can do. I hope you will come to see me if there are any more problems, Joanna. We are very pleased to have you in our school.'

It wasn't long before Joanna found herself at the top of standard five and a member of the choir. Some of the songs they sang were in Malay so Aniki had to help her with the words. Very soon the language became quite easy to understand and even the Chinese lessons were fun.

'Why did I hate everything so much?' Joanna asked Aniki, one afternoon as they floated in the shallow end of the pool.

'I don't know . . . I hated leaving Ipoh at first,' Aniki replied.

Joanna thought for a while and then she said:

'It all came right when I remembered that Jesus always cares for us even though we move away and forget him for a time.'

Aniki nodded. 'It is the same for me,' she agreed.

Joanna floated away and turned over into her clumsy

breaststroke. Once, twice, three times she ploughed across the breadth of the pool trying to do it without resting her feet on the bottom.

'You're not breathing properly and your arms are all out of time,' a well known voice jeered from the side.

Joanna stood up, hands on hips and glared at Philip who was still dry and clutching a towel. She felt the anger rising and the words that would cause an argument right there on the tip of her tongue but she bit them back.

Remember, she told herself, it takes two to fight!

'I know I'm doing it all wrong,' she agreed. 'How about helping me to get it right?'

The amazed look on Philip's face made her giggle and when he dumped his towel on a table and jumped in to join her they were both smiling.

'It was really good!' she told her mother that night. 'I was pulling back at the same time as I kicked and you should pause and then blow out. Philip says I'm quite fast now that I've got it right!'

'You seem to have got everything right, Joanna,' her father said, coming into the room to have his bow tie fastened, 'with a little bit of help!'

There was a big dance at the Officers' Mess and Mr and Mrs Lacey had dressed up for it.

'Oh, Mummy, you look beautiful,' Joanna sighed, and Aniki, who was staying the night, nodded in agreement.

Mrs Lacey was wearing a new dress. It was made of white silk and hung straight down from narrow shoulder straps that looked like strips of diamonds. She had piled her hair high on her head in a cluster of curls held with a diamond comb. Mr Lacey was in evening dress and had a white frill down the front of his shirt.

'Aren't I beautiful too?' he grinned.

Both girls nodded and giggled.

'Men are handsome, not beautiful!' Mrs Lacey said, linking her arm through her husband's and giving it a squeeze.

Joanna found she didn't mind a bit when they had gone. With Jaya and Aniki for company she had a lovely night.

'I'm really glad Mummy and Daddy are out!' she exclaimed as they started to clean up the kitchen after making coconut sweets, to Jaya's recipe. 'These sweets are very nice to eat but make a terrible mess!'

On Sunday morning the family went to the little church across the airfield. This time Joanna didn't notice the bare walls and the plastic chairs. She heard the stories and sang the hymns and when Mr James asked if she would sing a solo she smiled and said she'd love to.

'How would you like to go to the beach?' Mr Lacey asked as they walked back home after the service. 'I can borrow a friend's car this afternoon.'

Joanna jumped up and down with delight, not forgetting to ask if Aniki could go too. Jaya was visiting with her family so the four of them climbed into a rusty old Mini with a bag full of sandwiches and set off for the east coast.

'I haven't been further than school for ages!' Joanna announced as they passed the sprawl of buildings at Bukit Merah.

'It must be at least a whole month!' Mr Lacey said, his eyes twinkling at her through the rear view mirror.

As the car moved along with the traffic Joanna tried to look out at both sides at once, there was so much to see. A wide double carriageway ran down the centre of the island . . . called Bukit Timah Road on the way up and Dunearn Road on the way down. The two four-lane highways were divided by a wide drain, almost fifteen feet deep, that carried water down to the sea in the monsoon season. Aniki told Joanna all this as they passed by and went on describing all that they were seeing. Joanna knew that bukit meant hill and Aniki said that timah was the Malay word for tin and that once there had been a tin mine at Bukit Timah.

'Bukit Timah village sounds nicer than "Tin Hill" doesn't it?' Joanna said.

It took over an hour to get to the east coast, even though it was only sixteen or so miles, because the traffic was just as Joanna remembered it the day the taxi had driven them from the airport. The beaches were not crowded though. Joanna could see miles and miles of white sand stretching both ways into the distance and the sea was very still. There were one or two people in the sea, some of them with their clothes on, which Joanna found surprising, until she remembered how quickly her clothes had dried after the rainstorm.

It was a lovely day and the sea was warm, 'as warm as a bath' as Joanna had remarked. They were all careful to stay in the shade of the palm trees for most of the time, though, and not one of them was too sunburned at the end of the day. Mr Lacey took a different way home, driving along the south coast. They passed Clifford Pier which was right on the edge of the city skyscrapers and stopped to watch an old Chinese junk with red sails nosing out of the harbour on an evening cruise.

'Where is it going?' Joanna asked.

'Out to sea and round the islands of St John's and

Kusu,' Mr Lacey explained, 'and almost within sight of Sumatra.'

Joanna sighed. These were geography book names and here she was, actually living among them.

'Where are we now?' Mrs Lacey asked, as the car pulled to a stop in a large car park.

'Tiger Balm Gardens,' was the answer and the party trooped through the pagoda gateway. It was like a huge park but it was full of statues and figures out of Chinese legend and history all placed in scenes, like the pages of a picture book, among lovely trees and flowering shrubs. It was dark before they were half-way through the exhibition and Joanna was not happy at all in the section showing ancient tortures even though the place was floodlit.

'Ugh!' she said. 'Aren't they horrid!'

On the way home Mr Lacey told them about the Haw brothers who had built the garden and invented Tiger Balm . . . an ointment for every complaint.

'Mummy has some,' Joanna volunteered. 'She's had some for ages and I've read all about the Haw brothers. They have a big house in the city, full of jade carvings!'

'Well, now you've seen their gardens,' Mr Lacey said.

On Monday, at school, Joanna was told to report to a room next door to where she had Chinese lessons. When the teacher arrived it was the young one who had asked her name at the morning assembly.

'Come in, please. I am Miss Chen.'

Lots of small children were sitting in rows, their hair brushed down tidily and their white shirts and blouses gleaming in the Monday morning sun.

'Good morning, children,' Miss Chen said.

'Good morning, Teacher,' the children answered, as

though they were one person.

Joanna found herself smiling. They were so cute.

'Mr Toh has decided that it is silly for you to try to learn Mandarin so he suggests you help me for those periods each week.'

Joanna couldn't believe her ears. It was almost like being a teacher herself and she felt very proud.

'I thought perhaps you could teach them some English songs this morning,' Miss Chen suggested, moving to an old piano that stood against the verandah wall.

Joanna really enjoyed herself. She wrote 'The Grand Old Duke of York' on the blackboard and they loved it. Then they sang 'London's Burning' as a round and collapsed in giggles at the end.

'I'm going to teach them every week!' she told her mother as they had lunch together before a promised shopping trip to the city.

The Emporiums and Plazas were absolutely wonderful and Joanna thought back to that first night when she had thought they were ugly and noisy.

'How could I have been so silly,' she said, looking at the glass elevators rising to the fifth floor of Lucky Plaza. 'It all seems so different now.'

'I think you were wearing blue spectacles!' her mother said.

Joanna nodded.

'Blue or grey!' she agreed. 'I didn't want to like it, did I?'

Mrs Lacey took her hand and held it tightly.

'We all had to open our eyes, didn't we?' she said.

There was a lot of noise and commotion outside and Joanna and her mother hurried out on to the first-floor balcony to see what was happening. Down below them dozens of legs poked out from beneath a long dragon body made out of lengths of coloured material and at the front, held high on a stout pole, was a fearsome head which blew out puffs of smoke as it bobbed up and down. It had eyes that rolled and a mouth that opened and closed each time a cymbal crashed. There were acrobats and men on long stilts and strings of firecrackers that fizzed and spluttered then exploded with loud bangs.

'What is happening?' Joanna asked.

'I think it's a celebration for the start of the Chinese New Year,' Mrs Lacey said, leaning over the balcony to see the approach of two lions, their heads on long poles.

'But it's February!' Joanna exclaimed.

'That's right . . . that's when it is. Look!'

The two lions were poking their heads right up to the balcony rail and people were dropping dollar notes into the big mouths. Down on the pavement the long dragon was still weaving in and out of the crowds and young men were doing fantastic tricks with huge flags, waving and throwing them up into the air and catching them every time. They were very clever. Several young girls carried banners with Chinese characters on them and some had English-looking words too. 'KONG HEE FATT CHOI' they announced and Joanna supposed they said 'Happy New Year' or something very much the same.

Her day out ended at the bottom of Orchard Road where it divided into two, one road leading towards the east and Changi and the other straight down to the city proper. In the centre was a large grassy area with garden walks and flowering trees surrounding the cathedral.

Inside the cathedral Joanna felt it was impossible to

tell in which country she was. The interior had the same coolness and quietness that St Mark's had and she felt really at home. The cathedral was bigger than her own church but not as big as the minster at York where she had been with her mother one summer. Joanna wandered about the beautiful building, looking at the tall pillars, the vaulted roof and the flagstones of the nave, dappled with light from the stained glass in the great windows.

'Isn't it wonderful!' she sighed.

For a little while she sat in a pew in a side chapel and talked to Jesus as she used to do at home.

'How could I ever think you weren't here in Singapore?' she said. 'I was very silly, wasn't I? I know now that you are everywhere, in the little church by the airfield and even with me at the well.'

Joanna felt her mother's hand on her shoulder and looked at her.

'I know it's a lovely church,' she told her mother. 'But Jesus isn't only in places that are special. He's everywhere!'

Mrs Lacey smiled and nodded, not aware that Joanna was thinking about a deep cool cave well in a jungle kampong.

It was the day of the swimming gala and Joanna sat with her mother under a striped umbrella by the side of the deep end of the swimming pool. The swimming club were doing really well against that of the other Australian base across the island. Philip Kelly had already won the diving competition and the senior butterfly race.

'How are you feeling?' Mrs Lacey asked. 'You haven't

said a word for ten minutes.'

Joanna gulped. 'I'm a bit scared about my race,' she explained. 'I'm not all that good, you know!'

'I think it's splendid that you're swimming for the club. It's only been a couple of weeks since you joined.'

'I know it's because there's really no-one else,' Joanna said, 'but all I can do is my very best . . . so I'll try.'

Mrs Lacey smiled and gave Joanna's hand a squeeze.

'I'm sure you will,' she agreed.

Philip ran over to the table, dripping wet, and collapsed on the chair opposite Joanna.

'Phew!' he sighed. 'I really am tired. I couldn't swim another stroke. We only need two points for the championship so all you have to do is swim like mad and come second! First would be nice 'cos you'll get a certificate but second will do!'

'I feel really scared,' Joanna confessed quietly.

'What for? It's not *that* important!'

It is to me! Joanna said to herself.

Suddenly it was time for her to take her place in the shallow end. Because all the competitors were learners they were allowed to start in the water so that was easier for Joanna, who still hated diving or jumping in. She waited, her legs shivering and her mouth dry.

'On your marks . . .' the starter began, then Joanna took a deep breath and she was off. She tried to remember everything that Philip had told her. Pull back . . . kick . . . pause and breathe out. She had her eyes tightly shut so that the water wouldn't get in them and she couldn't hear because of the splashing all around her. Pull back . . . kick . . . pause and breathe out . . . she gasped to herself, trying with all her might to get it right.

Then almost before she had started she felt her hands touch the side and her arms were grabbed. She was pulled out of the water and on to the side. She could hear shouts and yells and hands were patting her on the back.

'Fantastic!' somebody said and Joanna could see that it was Philip when she managed to get the water out of her eyes.

'What?' she said, looking round in confusion.

'You won . . . you fantastic Pom!'

Joanna found herself surrounded by all the members of the club. Everybody had their arms round everybody else and they were all jumping up and down and shouting, 'We are the *greatest!*'

Right there in the middle of the bunch was a very happy Joanna Lacey.

'So you saved the day?' Mr Lacey said as they were having dinner that night.

'Yes,' Joanna nodded, 'but it was all the others who got the points. Philip won the diving and two races, as well as the last length of the relay. All I did was get a couple of points for swimming the breadth!'

'But they wouldn't have got the trophy without you, would they?' Mrs Lacey said.

Joanna shook her head.

'Team work?' she asked with a grin.

'Pulling together!' Mrs Lacey agreed.

That night Joanna settled at the table to write to Cathy and Anne. She hadn't felt like writing before because everything had been so awful, but she had to admit to herself now that it had been her own silliness that had caused most of it.

'Dear Cathy,' she began, then leaned back in her chair and chewed the end of her pen. How do you tell somebody in a cold wet place how lovely it is in the sun? she thought.

Dear Cathy,

How are you? I hope everything is all right at school. I miss everybody, especially you and Anne. Singapore is absolutely fantastic. Yesterday I helped the swimming club to win the Gala. I swim almost every day in the outdoor pool. School is great. I am top of the class in English and Maths and I'm teaching Standard One to sing English songs. I've sung solo in church too. Aniki and I go to see her grandmother who lives in a *real* jungle house. We go swimming to the beach too. Aniki likes my mother's cooking (even though our amah Jaya does most of it). I only go to school in the mornings but I stay on Tuesdays for choir practice. After school I swim or play tennis with Aniki. Sometimes we play squash at the officers' courts. I don't have to wash up or do anything like cleaning. I don't even have to make my own bed because Jaya does all that . . .

'What a strange letter from someone who *hates* Singapore!' Mrs Lacey said, leaning over Joanna's shoulder. '*That* Joanna seems to think it's a wonderful place!'

Joanna wrinkled her nose.

'This is the real Joanna,' she said. 'I don't know who the other one was. I didn't like her much!'

# Chapter Ten

A strange insect buzzed around her ears and Joanna tried to shoo it away with her hand. It really was very hot. There was a fan whirring around on the ceiling but her desk was right by the verandah wall and she couldn't feel any cool air at all. The sun was high in the sky and fell right on to her book and that made her eyes ache. The lesson seemed endless. She was supposed to be reading *Treasure Island* but she couldn't concentrate. Last time she had heard it read by Mr Brown with all his voices. Long John Silver didn't seem as exciting just read inside her head. There had been a long assembly that morning while Mr Toh told them about a National Courtesy Day which was to happen in May. There was a poetry competition but Joanna's head had started to ache and she hadn't paid much attention.

Now it was really hurting and she felt a little sick. At last, feeling worse and worse by the minute, she went to the front and spoke to Mrs DaSilva.

'Go and get a drink,' the teacher said.

Joanna sat in the canteen and sipped a carton of orange but her head still ached. When Aniki came out for break and joined her she widened her eyes and peered at her.

'You look *awful*!' she said.

It wasn't long before she was sitting on the bus on her way home. Mr Toh had made sure she could manage on her own and had spoken to the driver, asking him to keep his eye on her. She had insisted that there was no need to call her mother because Jaya was always at home.

'Here is your stop, Missy!' the driver called, leaning out of his cab.

The walk up to the bungalow seemed endless so Joanna took a short cut across the open ground, coming to the house at the back by the banana plants. Wearily she trudged along the back wall past the open living-room windows. She could hear her mother on the telephone as she stopped to rest, leaning her head on the hot red brick.

'I know that, darling!' she heard her mother say. It must be Daddy on the phone, Joanna thought. She didn't mean to listen in to the conversation but she was too weary to move. There was a long silence and then her mother's voice . . .

'When would we go? . . . How far is it? . . . What about school!'

Joanna's heart began to pound and she felt hotter and hotter as her stomach began to churn. Surely they were not moving again? Everything was spinning and she didn't make sense of anything until the name Aniki was mentioned, then she concentrated very hard and tried to pay attention.

'They are such good friends,' her mother was saying. 'It would be so sad to leave . . .'

Joanna didn't stay to hear any more. *Leave?* Surely they weren't going to leave? She stumbled across to Aniki's house and burst in through the kitchen door. Rafel and Mandhir were playing with a huge box of Lego on the floor and there was no sign of their mother.

'Aniki at school!' Mandhir announced.

'I know that,' Joanna answered. 'Can I wait for her to come home?'

'Aniki not come home . . . go grandmother with medicine,' Rafel added, leaning over and stealing a necessary piece of Lego from his twin.

Joanna ran from the fight that started immediately and headed for the main gate. If Aniki was going straight from school to Kampong Bungar then she would arrive at the same time.

The guards at the gate called to ask where she was going but she ignored them.

'I won't go!' she panted as she hurried down the narrow jungle paths. 'They can't make me. Not now, when I've made new friends and everything is all right. I won't go!'

She didn't remember the fork in the path.

'Oh, which way?' she wailed.

She chose the left hand path then wished she hadn't for the bushes and creepers got thicker and thicker.

'This is not the right way,' she sobbed, looking to right and left at the thick greenery. She looked behind her too and the path seemed to have disappeared altogether. At her feet a column of large black ants marched across the sandy path and she ran forward in case one of them bit her, like the one in her bedroom had on that first night.

Her school bag felt very heavy on her shoulder. Usually she only carried it from the bus into school and from the bus to the house. All kinds of things were jumbled together inside. Apart from her school books she had begun a diary, and a new box of crayons and a pen set had joined the red leather booklet. *The House at Pooh Corner* was in the bag too because she was reading it to Standard One and teaching them Pooh's songs. Piglet himself, back in his rainbow coat, was squeezed into the front pocket of the bag. He had made all the little ones laugh as they had passed him round while singing 'The more it snows, tiddly pom', one of Pooh's winter songs. All these things had made the bag quite heavy and Joanna's shoulder was very sore by the time she reached the clearing.

For a moment her heart leapt and a smile almost wrinkled the corners of her mouth then she gave a little cry and sank to her knees.

It was the wrong kampong!

The clearing was the same shape but it was littered with fallen leaves and dead branches and obviously hadn't been swept for a long time. The circle of houses, now that she looked closely, had great big holes in their roofs and doors were hanging off their hinges.

Joanna was very frightened. It was so quiet. Even the jungle sounds seemed to have stopped. She looked at her watch. It was only ten minutes past two and she should just be arriving home. It would be at least another hour before her mother began to worry because it was Tuesday when the choir had a practice.

'Well! I can't sit here,' she told herself, 'or the ants will eat me!'

She struggled to her feet, swung the heavy bag onto her shoulder again and approached the nearest house. One look inside the doorway showed her that the kampong was really abandoned. The place was full of huge cobwebs and a lot of scary rustling noises sent her down the steps and into the open again.

'Hello! Is there anybody there?' she called, but there was such a commotion of screeches and twitterings that she decided not to try that again.

Her head still ached and her throat was so dry and painful that it was hard to swallow. She felt just as she had done the last time she'd had the flu and the doctor had made her stay in bed. The thought of cool sheets and hot lemon made her sigh for cold English nights in her cosy pink and white bedroom, her big book open on her hunched-up knees, and Mummy sitting on the end of her bed with hot milky drinks. Then she thought of hot scented nights and iced Coca Cola at the restaurant in the village and shook her head.

'How can anybody love both things?' she asked the empty clearing.

The dryness in her throat made even breathing unpleasant so Joanna stopped feeling sorry for herself and looked around for a well, a cave-well, like the one in the grandmother's kampong or any other sort of well that might give her something to soothe her aching throat.

At the far side of the clearing she could see a pile of red bricks and started across the open space to investigate. Her legs were shaking but she wasn't sure whether it was because she was ill or because she was so scared. It was very lonely.

'What if nobody finds me?' she whispered, her heart

missing a beat. 'I'll just look for a drink then I'll try to find the way back!' she told herself sternly. 'The jungly parts of the island are only small!'

As she got nearer she could see that the pile of bricks was the remains of an 'igloo', just like the one that covered the cave-well in Kampong Bungar. With a little cry of relief Joanna ran towards it and the cool water she was sure was there under the ground.

'*Crack!*' The noise echoed around the deserted kampong followed by Joanna's cry as she disappeared in a flurry of rotten wood and dust. The jungle creatures jumped, flew, scampered and made their strange noises in answer. Then all was silent and the dust settled.

Joanna opened her eyes and groaned.

'Ooh!' she said, drawing in her breath as she felt the bump on her head that was adding to her headache. It took a few moments for her to remember where she was and when she did she began to cry. It was a cave-well, she had been right about that, but it was an empty one. The hollow where the water should be was a deep empty hole and the spring at the back of the cave was not flowing out of the rock. Looking up above her head, Joanna could see that the steps to this well had been wooden and that they had long since rotted away in the dampness of the jungle. Two steps remained, far above and out of reach, and she could see the broken board she must have fallen through, still half blocking the entrance hole. Trying to get to her feet brought such pain to her ankle that she sat down again and cried even harder, her sobs echoing around the dark hole she was sitting in.

The ankle was swollen and it was all just too much!

After a good long wail and a lot more miserable noises

Joanna dried her eyes on the edge of her tunic and had a good think.

'What would Mummy and Daddy do?' she asked herself.

She remembered the night when she had last visited the kampong with Aniki, how she had been in trouble at home, and how they had sat down as a family and made 'Good and Bad' lists.

'I'll do that now!' she decided.

While she was finding her rough-note book and a pencil that didn't need sharpening she found a packet of fruit pastilles, half empty and a bit grubby, at the bottom of her bag. Blowing the pencil shavings and lining fluff from the top one she popped it into her mouth and sighed.

'At last!' she muttered as the juicy sweet made her dry throat feel better. With some surprise she found that her headache had almost gone too!

'Bad things,' she wrote.

1. I'm in a hole in the ground and nobody knows where I am.
2. Nobody has been to this kampong for years and years.
3. My ankle hurts and I don't think I can walk.
4. It's getting dark!

Joanna was finding it difficult to see to write and looked at her watch, holding her wrist high to be nearer the hole in the roof and what little light was left. It was five-thirty and though it was never dark at that time she knew that the sun would have gone down behind the trees, putting the kampong in shadow.

I must have knocked myself out! she thought, beginning to shiver.

'Good things.'

She wrote the heading but for a moment couldn't think of anything good to write. She felt into one of the front pockets in her bag and popped another sweet into her mouth. At the same time she spied one of Piglet's ears poking out of the other pocket.

'We *are* in a mess!' she told him, pulling him out of the tight pocket and straightening his coat. Looking at him, the memories of Sundays and Kelly-Ann came flooding back. The rainbow coat she had put back on him when things had sorted themselves out reminded her of the last story Kelly-Ann had told her before she left England, how Joseph had been thrown into a pit by his brothers. She remembered Kelly-Ann's words, 'It all turns out fine, you know... Joseph was found!'

'And we'll be found too, Piglet!' she said with determination. 'Good things!'

1. I'm not really hurt except for my ankle.
2. Rafel will have told Daddy I went looking for Aniki.
3. Mummy and Daddy love me and will find me soon.
4. Jesus loves me and won't let anything bad happen to me.

'For,' she told Piglet, whom she could hardly see as it got darker, 'even the hairs on our heads are numbered... Dear Jesus, keep me safe until Mummy and Daddy find me. I know it was stupid to go running off and it's my own fault this has happened. Kelly-Ann told me all about making the best of things and how we are all special. Joseph didn't want to make his journey but because he did, his father and brothers were saved from starvation. I promise I'll make the best of whatever journey I have to make next, even if it means leaving here. Help me to stay myself wherever I am and whatever I'm doing.'

Two large tears ran down Joanna's cheeks as the last little bit of light left her hole in the ground. She was very frightened.

'But I'm not alone,' she sobbed. Then, holding Piglet close, she began to sing the song that Kelly-Ann had taught her that last day at Sunday school.

'I took Jesus for my Saviour,
You take him too . . .
Let his light shine on inside you,
All your life through . . .

As she reached the chorus Joanna felt much better and let her strong voice ring out.

'This little light of mine,
I'm gonna let it shine . . .'

She was singing so hard that she didn't hear the first shout but she heard the second one when a beam of light shone down from the opening.

'Joanna?' the familiar voice called.
'Daddy!' she answered.

'I was always sorry that I had never heard you sing a solo,' Mr Lacey said much later when Joanna was safely in her bed with her ankle bandaged up. 'I never thought I'd hear it coming up out of the ground in the middle of the jungle!'

'I always said I was glad I can sing,' Joanna grinned. Everything had been sorted out and explained. Aniki was sitting on the edge of Joanna's bed beaming all over her face and Mr and Mrs Lacey left them together. They weren't angry, much to Joanna's surprise. They were far too relieved for that and quite understood how such a mistake was easy to make. For a mistake it was. All that Mrs Lacey had been talking about on the telephone was a holiday. A wonderful two weeks on Penang Island, right up the Malaysian Peninsular, and Aniki was to go too.

'I really did get it all wrong, didn't I?' Joanna said, rubbing her forehead where a large lump had appeared. 'But you got it right, Aniki, thank goodness!'

Aniki grinned.

'When Rafel said you had run off to find me I knew you would try to find Kampong Bungar. I only took your Daddy to the fork in the path then I came back,' she explained.

'How did you know which path I had taken?'

Aniki held up a crumpled bit of yellow paper.

'Your bus ticket!' she said.

They both laughed.

'Saved by a bus ticket!' Aniki said.

Joanna nodded, settling down into her pillow with a sigh.

'A bus ticket, a very special song and a rainbow coat of many colours,' she said.

Aniki looked confused but Joanna just grinned.

'Tomorrow I'll tell you a story,' Joanna said, glancing at the story Bible that sat in her basket chair. 'In fact, I'll tell you lots of stories when we are on our holiday!'

Joanna watched the chit-chat run up the wall and across the ceiling.

'Are you the same lizard that scared me so much on my first day here?' she asked sleepily.

His tail waved slowly from side to side.

'I don't suppose you are, but that's fine. I'm not the same Joanna that screamed at you either.'

The little creature disappeared behind the wooden window frame and Joanna sighed.

'We're both at home,' she murmured as she fell asleep.